S. K. ARNETTE

Hidden Bones

Levi, I should have been writing this one with you.
Miss you.

Contents

Foreword

Acknowledgement

I don't know where I would be without my husband. He has supported me, loved me, and put up with hearing about a thousand stories for a couple of decades now. I'm hoping for several more to come.

Book Club Buddies!! Love you guys! Thanks for putting up with me taking over book club to talk about my writing.

I

Part One

Prologue — The House

1913

The house is finally built. It seemed to take a long time for John and Hilda Miller. The house was John's wedding present to Hilda, his lovely wife of two years now. They had spent the last two years living with his parents, practicing a level of patience that should recommend them for sainthood.

Mr. Miller was always bringing home his work buddies to see his soon-to-be-famous lawyer son. Mrs. Miller was constantly dragging Hilda from one banquet to another, from one luncheon to another. Meanwhile, John Miller just wanted to relax and get to know his new wife. Hilda just wanted to find some solitude to read her books and plan her new home. They both learned a lot about patience during those two years.

Finally, though, the house is built. It is a large, red brick home. It stands taller than any of the neighboring homes, taller even than the doctor's home next to it. It is what is known as a Four-Square design, solid and square. Nothing short of a cataclysmic, natural disaster could stand a chance to bring down the house. It has the clean lines that are the rage this decade. The plants in front of the porch draw the eye up to the house, creating a stage for the porch that they stand in front of. They are leafy, non-flowering plants that promise to look good the entire season with a minimum of work required to maintain them. They will even look good next year without needing to be replanted. They include two different types of hostas. Spiderworts and lilies, the only blooming flowers of the bunch, were added to give the garden some much-needed color.

The inside is just as impressive as the outside. The hardwood floors are the first thing you notice. They are bright with wax and shine in the sunlight that the large windows let in. The rooms are large, with pocket doors separating them and ensuring that the living room and dining rooms are warm in the winter, trapping the heat from the central fireplace. The kitchen is also separated from the rest of the house with a pocket door. This would be vital when they were entertaining and wanted some privacy. In the winter they would also help to keep the kitchen warm, and in the summer they would help to keep the living room cool.

The kitchen was a work of art in itself. There were cabinets covering almost every wall. There were what felt like miles worth of counters, and even a small kitchen nook for the servants to enjoy their meals. The pantry was a thing of absolute beauty, with shelves and shelves worth of space to keep the non-perishable staples of the home. No expense was spared in the downstairs of the home.

The private areas were a little tighter than the downstairs. The rooms were smaller, but even they were warm and comfortable. Here is where cost-saving measures were implemented. Even then, the hallway was wide, and the rooms were warm. There were a lot of rooms in the upstairs area, a total of four bedrooms. The Millers had hope of a couple of children to grace their home. Those rooms found later use as a sewing room, an office, and a guest room.

The attic was well-designed, just like the rest of the home. The storage spaces were lined with shelves. There was even a small room up there for the servants if they chose to live in the house, rather than outside of it. The stairs there were steep, and there was a 180-degree turn on the landing, but there were not a lot of stairs. It was possible to lift things from the bottom step, right up to the attic floor without having to carry them up the stairs. There was a metal railing preventing people from falling from the attic to the stairs when one was not moving things into or out of the attic.

The walls in the home were thick. This came in handy when John Miller began to run his law business out of the small office in his home. He took a page out of his doctor neighbor's book, and set up a seating area in the foyer, allowing the clients to sit in relative comfort while they wait to talk with him about their legal problems. It was not uncommon for the doctor and Mr. Miller to have some of the same clients.

The home location was strategic. The home was two blocks off of the strip known as Millionaire's Row. They were able to enjoy the beauty and the luxuries of their more well-to-do neighbors, while not taking on the costs of the homes on that street. That also meant that most of the clients seen by the doctor and the lawyer were the workers who serviced those homes. This kept the two families abreast of the latest fashions and parties. Life was perfect.

1974

The house was a steal. Robin McGuire was able to purchase the old brick home for pennies to the dollar of what the home was worth. The lawyer, John Miller, who had owned the home died, leaving no heirs to the property. The house had sat empty for a few years after that. Yeah, the old house was going to need some work, but that's what happens when buying from a city auction.

The hardwood flooring could stay, but the walls needed repainting. The pocket doors needed to come out, opening the house up a bit. Old houses like this one were often over-engineered, placing walls where there did not need to be walls. The open floorplan was much more the rage, anymore The cabinet design was good, but the cabinets needed to be replaced. The countertops needed to be updated, as well. The kitchen floor needed to be redone. The stairs and upstairs bedrooms needed to be recarpeted, but they were in good repair. This would be an easy home to clean up and rent out.

It took most of 1974, but Robin McGuire was finally able to say that the house looked great. It was warm and inviting, perfect for his first renters. The home was perfect, but Rob McGuire found that he had a hard time finding renters for the home. It was just too big. Most families that could fill the home bought their own home, rather than renting a house.

Coming upon desperate times to get the home filled with renters before he came forced to sell it, he lowered the price of the rent. It was just enough for Teddy Koonz and his wife Kitty to be able to afford it. It was less than a month before they moved in, excited to share their new home with their young daughter, Annie. It would be just over a year before they moved out, this time without their beloved Annie. The house got to keep their young daughter, making up for all the years of longing that its former mistress expressed.

Home — 2007

"It is finally ours!" Maggie screamed as she pulled the U-haul box truck into the driveway of an old, red brick house. Peter, her husband sitting next to her promptly sticks his finger in his ear with an exaggerated grimace. Maggie is not a particularly quiet individual at the best of times. This is a particularly loud moment for her. He was expecting it though. They had worked long and hard to be able to afford a house of their own.

"Yes, it is finally ours," he says with a smile after his ears stop ringing from Maggie's excitement. He is much quieter than she is, although no less excited. "It's your house, too!" he says with a smile, as he ruffles the ears of the big pitbull mix at his feet. "You were the last one to move into our old apartment, and now you're the first one to move into our new house! You even have a yard you get to play in."

River, the pitbull/german shepherd mix, is the baby of the family. She was the primary reason the young couple were moving. While she had lived in apartments her entire life, they wanted to give her the best of everything, and a yard to play in was part of that best life. So was the peace and quiet that one finds when they own their own home and do not have to deal with neighbors.

The annoying neighbor downstairs who spent the nights screaming and the days blasting music so loud that it echoed down the street had nothing to do with looking for a new home, at all. At least that is what they tell themselves, and never mention to their friends. No one ever wants to admit that they have been forced out of their home by someone else.

They had tried everything to deal with the man. They tried talking to him, reasoning with him, talking to his family, and even tried the police. Nothing seemed to help for more than a couple of days. Finally, it had been too much for them. So under the pretense of looking for a house with a yard for River, they gave up the apartment that they had been living in for the past ten years.

The house itself is a red brick American Foursquare. It has a large front porch, painted in yellow and blue, setting off the red brick beautifully. There is a back deck that had been added on later, but the porch was original to the house. The windows were new, but the frames were original slate. The roof is new, but the decorative wood dates back to the original building in 1913. It was the perfect blend of old and new designs working to create a beautiful home. With five bedrooms, a deep yard, and a single-car garage, it was a steal of a home.

It had cost thousands less than other comparable houses in the area. The previous owner was getting out of the home renting business, sticking only to apartments. He had said it was simply too expensive to rent out a home to people when buying it was so much cheaper. Considering that their mortgage was less than what they had been paying renting a two-bedroom apartment, the Reeds were inclined to agree with him.

Pulling around to the back, Maggie and Peter prop open the gate leading to the house and start carrying in the hundreds of boxes that they seem to have accumulated in the ten years that they have been married. River hung out in the basement as they moved, enjoying the blue cement flooring and all of the new smells, not that she had ever inclined to wander. She was seldom more than six feet away from Maggie. Not that it was worth the risk that something might distract River and cause her to get lost. She was too important to Maggie and Peter to even consider risking.

They had decided on doing all of one load today, and the rest will be the following day. After all, they got a late start today, seeing as they had to be at the lawyer's office at ten in the morning to sign for the house. While the television shows make that look like a five-minute transaction, Maggie was pretty sure that they lost days in there, with the reading of the contract and the small talk between the agents, lawyers, and the seller.

It had been a stressful event. The mortgage company that they had used had withheld some of the vital documents they needed until the very last moment. They said it was to ensure that the Reeds were not being pressured into buying a house. The Reeds were pretty sure that someone just forgot to fill out some paperwork. Either way, Maggie was on the phone with the mortgage company as they walked into the lawyer's office, making sure that the paperwork arrived in time for the signing. The lawyers that they were meeting with were impressed with how fast she was able to get the paperwork to come through the fax machine once she started talking. She was not even off the phone before the paperwork started coming in.

That first load that was moved in was just kitchen stuff, bathroom stuff, and bedding. Just what they needed to survive their first night in the new home. There were boxes of pots, pans, and cooking utensils, but no food, except for food for River. There were toilet paper, soap, and towels, and shower curtains. They had bedding, but no bed and no extra clothing. At least they had a coffee maker, filters, and grounds. They were bare bones living in their new home for the moment. It was surprising how many boxes all of that had taken to move.

As they finished setting up the kitchen, for the moment anyway, Peter could not help but take a good look at his wife. Maggie Reed stood all of five feet, weighing a healthy 150 pounds. She was more muscular than fat, with a flatter stomach and strong legs. She looked at home in the house already. She had her auburn hair tied in a messy ponytail behind her, and she was leaning against the white counters as though she could not be happier. Clutching her first coffee, in the only mug she brought, in their new home, she smiled and closed her big, brown eyes.

Peter was almost the exact opposite of Maggie. Peter was taller than her by an entire foot. While Maggie had a little bit of weight on her, Peter was lean and defined. His blond hair was no longer thick, rather thinning out on the top, not that you notice his hair with how short he keeps it. His blue eyes were open. He did not clutch a coffee cup, but rather an energy drink. It had been a long day. He needed the caffeine.

"We should order pizza and then lay down some blankets to sleep on. River is going to love us sleeping on the floor with her," Maggie suggested. She did not need to look at him to know he was still in the room. She could feel him. She could also feel River at her feet, dancing at the idea of pizza.

"Lies, River has not slept on the floor in 10 years. She is going to be pissed to sleep on the floor, even if it is with us. She will demand her bed, that she sometimes lets us sleep in," Peter laughed as he responded as he pulled his phone from his pocket. Maggie might be wrong about River's sleeping preference, but she was right about the pizza. That sounded delicious.

Pepperoni pizza from the small diner, Pips, was perfect. The night spent sleeping on the floor, with a couple of quilts between them and the carpet, in what they decided was their room, was less than enjoyable. River, contrary to Peter's belief, loved it. She was the only one who got good sleep. Maggie and Peter were left wondering what happened to those days when they could fall asleep comfortably on just about any semi-horizontal spot and wake up feeling amazing.

While Maggie might not have loved sleeping on the floor and outright hated the cold shower, *I'll be fixing that issue as soon as possible.* She adored the quiet of the house, so different than living in the apartment had been. The creaks and sighs of a house getting used to new people living in it were oddly comforting. It reminded her of her old childhood home. It was big and older, although not as big or as old as this one. She pulled back her hair as she bounced down the stairs, feeling like a kid again, living in a giant house.

She grew up in one not that far away from where they were living now. This house was not dissimilar to the one she grew up in. The big difference was that she grew up in a wooden house, and this one was brick. She likes the stability of the brick houses over the wooden ones. When the wind blew, the old wooden houses would rock and shake. The brick ones never budge, allowing you the comfort of forgetting about the weather outside, and sheltering you from the worst the world can throw at you. She crosses the living room, and the dining, without a care in the world but what to load up and move for the day.

That changed when she hit the kitchen.

Home — 1975

Annie is so excited! It is her very first house. Her mom, dad, and she had always lived in shabby, little apartments, and now she is going to live in a giant house. Not that she understood that any of the apartments were shabby. That was just what Dad said right before they moved. The house even has a yard for her to play in. Maybe she could get a puppy. She has always wanted a puppy.

At eight years old, Annie is the picture of life and joy. Her bright blond hair springs around her face in the best Shirley Temple curls ever, and they are all-natural. She did not even need the rag rollers to get the perfect curls. She never pays attention to them, but she likes that her Mom fusses over her curls. Her blue eyes are shining like a summer day's sky. Her cheeks are chubby and pink. She is wearing her favorite blue dress and her saddle shoes are polished. It is the best day of her life.

Annie did not have a lot that she was expected to do with the move. She is pretty small, even for an eight-year-old. Most of her classmates are a good head taller than her, and they all outweighed her. Annie is thin. What she lacked in size, she more than made up in brains and speed though. She is always the first one done with her classwork, and she can run faster than even the biggest boy in her class. None of this was very helpful in the moving process though.

She did pack her own stuff for the move. She even helped Mom pack up a few boxes. She made sure to put the heaviest things at the bottom of the box, and lighter things that are related to the first things went next. Finally, she learned to fill in the box with small items, using as much room in the box as possible. The first few times she did this, she made the boxes too heavy, but she quickly figured out, with Mom's help, how to pack the boxes.

The biggest help that she could be was quiet and out of the way while her parents did the heavy lifting. Annie is very good at being quiet and out of the way. She is used to entertaining herself. She is an only child and since her Mom worked, she is often left alone to take care of herself. She would just have to be careful today, she was wearing her favorite dress and she did not want it to get dirty.

While Mom and Dad carried boxes into the house from the back of Dad's truck, Annie keeps herself occupied in the backyard. She has some chalk and the entire side of the garage that she can draw on. She had asked Mom if it was okay. Mom said it was okay, so long as she stayed quiet and out of the way while they worked. That was an easy promise for Annie to make and an easy one for her to keep.

Mom and Dad had started moving early in the morning. So early that the sun had barely risen. They filled the truck bed at the old apartment, and then emptied it at their new home, with Teddy taking things out of the truck bed and handing them to Kitty at the kitchen door. It was a system that they had perfected through all the times that they had moved before.

By the time it is noon, Annie is very hungry. She had missed breakfast, being too excited to see her new home. Luckily for her, Mom had come prepared. She is always prepared for just about everything. Annie has never seen her flustered by anything, even when Dad was upset about something. She is a quick thinker and a good planner.

The tiny family sits in the backyard, under the shade of the tree that reached over the garage. From its leaves, Annie can tell it is a maple tree. She will have to remember to see if she can get syrup from it in the fall. From a small styrofoam cooler, Annie's Mom, Kitty, pulls out a loaf of bread. Well, it looks like a loaf of bread anyway. Instead, it is an entire loaf of bread that has been prepared into sandwiches. Every set of slices had a filling of chicken salad in it, and then it was placed back in the loaf bag. Kitty also pulls out a can of soda for Annie and one for herself, and a can of beer for Dad, Teddy. She hands out paper towels, but she did not have any paper plates. Instead, Annie has to set her sandwich on the towel, but that was okay.

Dad decides to take a quick nap before continuing the hard work of moving stuff, so Mom decides to take Annie for a walk. There is no sense in disturbing Dad. Annie certainly knows better than to anyway. Sometimes Mom had to wake Dad, but Annie never did. Nothing good ever came from waking him up, not that he was ever intentionally mean to Annie. After all, he loved her and he cried when he hurt her, so she knew that he really meant it when he said that he loved her and that he was sorry.

In silence, mother and daughter got up from their little picnic, and start down the long driveway. The driveway looks almost new. The cement is straight, and there are no cracks. It is the perfect driveway for a perfect house. It was not until they got out to the front yard, that Mom spoke. "What do you think of it, so far?"

"Well, I haven't really seen the inside of the house yet, but the backyard is nice. The grass is so soft on my feet. The tree gives so much shade. I love it," Annie answers after a moment's thought. She likes how cool the backyard felt in comparison to the last place they lived. Last time, the only yard she had to play in was actually the cement parking lot behind their apartment building that they shared with five other families. There was no shade except for when the sun was behind the building. The cement was hot under her feet and it was not very fun to play there. Plus she had to be constantly on the lookout for cars.

"Have you gone on the deck, yet?"

"No, I did not want to be in your guys' way. I stayed by the garage the whole time. I drew on the garage wall, read a book, and played with my Dolly. It was the best time. Dolly wants to know if we are going to get a puppy." Dolly is named after Dolly Parton, one of Dad's favorite singers. The fact that Dolly was also a baby doll is a matter of mere coincidence that only amuses Annie more.

Mom laughs at that, "No, I don't think we're gonna get a dog. We don't own this house. We're just renting it. I don't think the landlord will let us have a dog in the house. It would not be fair to the dog to leave it tied up in the backyard all day because it was not allowed in the house, now would it?"

"We would have to leave the dog outside, even in the winter?"

"Yep, even in the winter. Even when it is snowing or raining. That wouldn't be fair."

"No, I don't think that would be very fair to the dog. Maybe one day, when we own our own house I can have a dog?"

"Maybe one day," Mom agrees. They turned left once they reached the sidewalk, but Annie had not been paying attention. She is too focused on her Mom and holding her hand. Annie loves holding her Mom's hand. It is not until they stood at the corner, about to cross the street that Annie looks around.

The street is lined with trees, including a beautiful golden tree. It looks like a tree straight out of her stories. The street is one way, but Mom said that she always had to look both ways before crossing the street, every single time even if the traffic is supposed to be in only one direction. After looking, Mom leads Annie across the street and down the next block. There, Annie sees the best view yet, a park.

"When you get older, you can come down here on your own. But for right now, I will need to go with you when you want to visit the park, do you understand?" Mom explains.

"Yes, you need to come with me to the park. I cannot go alone until you tell me that I'm old enough," Annie answers. She likes to rephrase what Mom and Dad tell her. It helps her to remember their instructions.

"Right. But, now that we are here, have fun! Run and play! I'll be right here on this bench until it is time to go."

Annie did just that, running around, pretending to play hide and seek between the trees for a while. She then takes her time and investigates all of the flowers that were planted in the center of the park. She did not pick any though. She likes to leave plants where they grow so that everyone can enjoy them. She chases the squirrels and runs around, laughing with delight. She loves her new home.

The Cabinets — 2007

Maggie wakes up bright and early after a night of sleeping on the floor with Peter and River. It was not the best night of sleep that she had ever had, but to be honest, it was very far from the worst. There was one time in college when Maggie had slept in her dorm building's stairwell. She had somehow managed to lose her key and her roommate was not home to let her in. In the morning she discovered that key in her back pocket, which she swore that she had checked. Her neck and back had hurt for a week, and her legs felt like they had been asleep for a year. That was a rough night.

Peter gets up shortly after Maggie did, thanks to some prodding from River. River much prefers everyone to stay together, all of the time. She is happiest when she needs only to move her head to see her two favorite people in the world. If she could not have that, then she was going with Mom and Dad could fend for himself.

While Maggie hops in the shower, Peter gets dressed. He heard Maggie's yip of surprise when she got in the shower. "Are you okay?" he calls out to her. He had not heard her fall, but maybe she stubbed her toe or stepped on something. Lord help them both if it was a spider or some other bug.

"Yeah, I'm good. You're gonna love the shower, it's nice and hot," Maggie calls back through the closed door. When she got out of the shower much quicker than normal, he began to question her honesty in that regard.

"The shower is super hot?" Peter asked her, reaching over to touch her red skin. It is ice cold.

"Super hot, hottest shower ever," Maggie replied. Standing right in front of him, Peter could clearly see she was being sarcastic.

"I bet they have the hot water tank turned down to conserve energy before selling the house. We can fix that. There is no reason for ice-cold showers, although that might have been the fastest shower I have ever seen you take," Peter assures her, while he pulls her close to warm her up. Maggie is well-known for her lava-like showers, and for taking her time enjoying getting cooked like a lobster. A shower in under five minutes is unheard of from her.

"Oh good, because I will not be doing that again. That was the worst shower ever. That was even worse than the not shower I had after Matt swore that the RV Park had running water and I had to bathe in a bucket after that marathon." Maggie relaxes into Peter's embrace, happy to be warm and comfortable, even as she remembered not being so comfortable after running a marathon that her brother convinced her to run with him. Bloody Matt. She will never let him live that down.

Matt and Maggie are both runners, him being much more into running than she is. Matt begged her to run a marathon with him in Cleveland. It was going to be a great time, the best time. She said she would go, on one condition. Wherever they stayed, there had to be running water. That meant flushing toilets and showers. She had camped without those luxuries when they were kids, but as an adult, she wanted just those two items from their trip.

Matt had a pop-up camper and made reservations for a campsite. Trusting her baby brother, Maggie did not even check, she just agreed. There was no running water. There were pit potties and a well. Twenty-six miles later that weekend, as she washed in a bucket beside the pop-up, she vowed to do the reservations herself from now on. It will be an inside joke in the family for the rest of their lives, and maybe into the next one.

"Worse than that shower in that state park in Montana? With the mosquitoes the size of small birds?" Peter asks, blanking on the state park in question.

"You mean, White Fish Lake?" Maggie pulls away a little bit to look up at Peter. "Um, it might be a tie between those two showers," she answered, tucking her head back against his chest. That had been a family trip, with everyone before her siblings started making kids. That was a nightmare shower, too. The mosquitoes had taken to breeding in the shower stalls, and they were huge. She took one shower there for the entire week that they had stayed. It was one shower too many.

Warm, dry, and smiling about that little adventure she had with her brother, Maggie went downstairs to let River outside to go potty and to make herself a pot of coffee. She did not notice the problem when she first walked through the kitchen with River at her heels. It was only when she went to open the cabinet where she put her coffee supplies that she noticed it. Every single cabinet door was open, even the ones that they did not touch the night before.

"Peter?" Maggie calls to her husband.

Hearing the tension in his wife's voice, he did not answer, but rather just went to where she was, the kitchen. "What's up?"

"Look at the cabinets. They are all open." Maggie gestures around the kitchen, pointing out the cabinets that were all open a slight bit. None of them were wide open. They were just a couple of inches open, enough to clearly not be latched.

"So? We must not have fully closed the cabinets last night. The house might have settled a bit and the cabinet doors moved. It's no big deal," Peter reasoned. Peter is good at coming up with logical reasons for things.

"We did not touch some of these cabinets, though."

"Then the realtor or the inspector did not close the cabinets. If it keeps happening, we will just get new magnets for them or some other latch. The cabinets are old, I am sure some of the hardware is worn out."

"Maybe..." Maggie is not convinced. She could have sworn that if nothing else, she closed the cabinet where her coffee supplies were. She always made sure that wherever she put the coffee supplies was well shut. She did not want to find bugs in her grounds. She would probably rage, but she would definitely cry if she found that. Not to mention that Peter would never let her forget it.

But maybe Peter is right and the hardware was just worn out. He is probably right. He usually is. It is not like it could have been a ghost or anything. Those do not exist, and besides, if they did have a spirit in the house, surely it has better things to do than open cabinets and try to scare them. She has just been reading too many scary stories and watching too many horror movies. That was it. Nothing to be worried about at all. Nothing at all.

"Yeah, you're right, of course. Well, let's get this show on the road. We have a lot of stuff to move and only a limited time with the moving truck," Maggie said with a forced smile on her lips.

Once River is done going potty, Maggie fed her. River eats a kibble and fresh food mixture that is designed to help her coat and prevent allergy attacks. River is allergic to wheat grain, making it a little harder to get the best food for her. Once River finishes her food, Maggie let her back out once again, and starts planning for the rest of the move. Maggie loves to plan things out, and her plans often work. As she stands at the kitchen counter, pen and coffee cup in hand, Peter could not help but be just a little awed in his wife. She could handle anything, including th buying of this house and the subsequent move, and she could handle it with grace. When she is ready, Maggie brought River back in the house, and lead her to the basement. It is the safest spot for her to be if they were going to be opening and closing the doors all day. River did not mind, there is a lot of stuff to sniff down there.

Exploring — 1975

Annie has the best time exploring the park that was only a couple blocks from her new home. It is a nice park, filled with trees and soft, green grass. There is a school that was across the street. Annie has a pretty good idea that it was going to be the school she would go to next term. There are sidewalk paths that formed a star-like pattern, leading to a small central garden. Bright and fragrant flowers have been planted there by the local gardening club, and they sway lightly in the breeze.

There are convenient benches scattered along the paths. There are squirrels, chipmunks, and birds all going about their business, completely unconcerned about the small human in their midst. There are even people walking their dogs along the park paths. A couple of the dog owners even let little Annie pet their dogs. Her favorite was the tiny poodle who was able to jump as high as she was tall. He made her laugh with the silly tricks that he did at his owner's request. It makes her want a dog more than ever, but asking again would only get her in trouble for pestering.

There is a second half of the park, but that is across the street from where she is with her Mom. It has a large playground and what looks like an outside classroom set up. "Can we go over there?" Annie asks when she approached her Mom. Kitty has been crocheting, while Annie played. Kitty trys to always bring her handwork with her when she is outside, relaxing. She likes how the handwork is mildlessly mindful, if that makes any sense to anyone but her. She could focus on the blanket or scarf she is making without having to fully ignore the rest of the world, Annie in particular.

"Hum? Oh, to the other side? No, I think we will have to visit that on a different day. Come on, we should be getting back. Your Dad will be upset if we let him sleep the whole afternoon away. I know he wants to get most of our stuff moved today," Kitty answers while she packs up her crochet stuff. Annie had not noticed her grab it when they left the backyard. She likes to watch her Mom make things out of nothing but a ball of yarn, using nothing more than a small hooked stick. It was like magic.

Taking Kitty's hand, Annie and Kitty walk back home, using the same route that they took to get there. Annie likes it when they go different routes every time they came and went somewhere, but with the park being so close, it make more sense to go the same route. Maybe next time they could explore a different way, maybe turning right at the end of the driveway instead of left.

Once they get home, Kitty sends Annie towards the house. "Why don't you explore inside for a few minutes. Pick out a bedroom that you think you might like to sleep in. Your Dad and I will be right back after we pack up some more stuff." Kitty watchs Annie until she is safely in the house with the door closed. Then she approaches Teddy to wake him up.

Teddy tends to swing when he wakes up. It is a side effect of his time in the Vietnam War. Teddy was a softy who never lost his temper before he was drafted. They had gotten married as soon as he found out that he was to be drafted. They had planned on a large wedding before he was drafted, but settled on a small district of the justice wedding, like so many of her friends. Time and money were in short supply. Teddy shipped out within a month of them getting married. She did not know she was pregnant with Annie, yet. The man who returned was not the same one that she married.

While she longs to reach over and wake Teddy with a kiss, just like the fairy tales she read when she was a child, Kitty knows better. Instead, she goes towards his feet. Teddy is stretched out on his back, one hand on his chest, and the other draped over his eyes. His legs are slightly spread apart, and he is still wearing his shoes. It is those shoes that Kitty lightly tapped with the toe of her shoes.

Teddy's reaction is swift and violent. He immediately jumps up and thrashes his arms. She knows from experience that this is normal in him now, and she knew from her friends, that their husbands sometimes did this too. She holds still, waiting patiently until he realized where he was and that there was no threat. Once he looks up to her, she offers him her hand to help him up. Her smile is tight, she worries that one day he would accidentally hit her, or worse, hit Annie, with his wild thrashings.

Standing, Teddy looked down into his wife's eyes. "What time is it?" he asks her. He no longer wears his watch after accidentally breaking it at work.

"Just after two. Annie is inside playing. If we hurry, we might be able to get a few more loads done before it gets too dark to see," Kitty answers him. With a nod from him, they both head off to finish packing and loading the rest of their belongings. They do not have a lot, so they are hoping to have it all done by the end of the day.

***

Annie is used to being left alone to fend for herself. She often came home from school to an empty house. Mom works as a housekeeper and is out for long periods of time, cleaning everyone else's house. Dad works in a forge, swinging a hammer. Annie is not sure what that actually means, but that is what Dad told her that he did. She knows the rules, do not open the door to anyone. Do not leave the house. Do not play with fire. They are easy rules to follow, and so far nothing bad has happened.

Annie goes from room to room in the house, trying to decide on the best bedroom to claim as her own. They are all almost the same size, except for the attic room. That one is almost half of the third floor. That would be her playroom. She chooses the bedroom right at the front of the house on the left side. It has two windows and overlooks the street. With two windows, she would not need to use her light to read by, she could use the sun. The best part is that the windows are big enough for her to sit in, so she would make a seat out of them and read her books to her heart's content. She sits down in the one overlooking the street and begins to daydream of all of the adventures she would enjoy between the pages. It is a pleasant daydream.

The Doll — 2007

I t has been a full month of living in their new home, and Maggie and Peter could not be happier. Whatever was going on with the cabinets has not happened again, saving them from having to replace all the hardware on their cabinets. Not that they have not been looking at eventually replacing them. The kitchen looks like it has not been renovated since the 1970s.

What the Reeds did not know is that the kitchen had literally not been renovated since the 1970s, when Robin McGuire bought the house. He paid a lot of money making a nice kitchen, and that kitchen had held up through various renters. The fact that the hardware and cabinets had lasted so long is a testament to their quality.

Peter is more than happy to claim the win about the kitchen. Ghosts do not exist, there is no way that it was some spirit is in their house, messing with their cabinets. That type of stuff simply did not happen in real life. It is the stuff of fantasy and television. That is not to say that he did not hesitate when looking at the cabinets now and again, and check twice when he closed them.

He occasionally did leave one or two of them open, to tease Maggie. She would get excited every time that he left a cabinet partially open and come running to him to show him. Every time, he would pretend to be amazed that the cabinet is open, only to give himself away by smiling and laughing. Maggie always pretends to hate it, but he knows she loves his teasing by the way she would turn and try to hide her smile.

Peter likes to tease Maggie, in a good-hearted way. One time, as they were unpacking the rest of Maggie's seemingly millions of mugs, he placed all of them on the top shelf, where he knew she could not reach them. It might have gone over better if she had her coffee before discovering that she could not reach the mugs, but it was still funny. Maggie even cracked a smile once he reached her coffee mug for her.

It was because of Peter's frequent teasing that when she discovered a doll sitting on the back steps, Maggie did not immediately freak out. She just assumes that Peter put it there to scare her. After all, it was certainly a creepy doll, and they did just watch the movie Chucky.

The doll is a stereotypical baby doll, obviously worn and dirty with age. There are dirt and leaves ground into what was once blond hair, now white with age and discoloration. The face iss filthy and the dress is in tatters. The dress may have been blue at one time, but now it is impossible to tell. The doll looks like it had lived outside for thirty years. The eyes still worked though, opening and closing when Maggie picked up the doll, tilting it to get a better look. She almost swears it made a noise when she set it back on the stairs.

"Where did you get that creepy doll?" Maggie asks Peter, meeting him in the kitchen. She had been picking up food, not feeling like cooking that day. She begins to wash her hands while she waits for his answer. She is not eating her tacos after touching that dirty doll without washing her hands first.

"What creepy doll?" Peter does not sound like he is teasing her. He sounds perplexed.

"The one that you put on the stairs. You did put a creepy baby doll on the stairs to scare me, right?" Maggie's voice is wary, certain that something creepy is going on now.

"No. Where would I have gotten a baby doll?" Peter is not teasing. He is serious. Crossing the kitchen he opens the door quickly, almost as though he expects to see some kids playing games on them. Instead, he is greeted by a baby doll, sitting on the deck, facing the door.

"What the hell is this?" Peter asks, almost demanding of Maggie.

"That's the baby doll that I found on the stairs. But I left it on the stairs. What is it doing on the deck?" Maggie answers after walking over to Peter. She is still drying her hands with a towel. She clutches at that towel as she looks over at the doll which had somehow made its way up three stairs and managed to turn around, staring at them. By the sound of the tension in her voice, Peter knows that she is not joking with him. She had really left it on the stairs and it appears to have moved on its own.

"I'm getting rid of it. It is going in the trash," Peter announces. He is doing his best not to show any fear of the doll. If he got nervous about it, Maggie would get nervous about it. Especially since they watched that stupid movie about that stupid doll, Chucky. She had gotten scared, and even mentioned how glad she was that they did not have dolls. She even told him about the dolls that her Mother used to have at her Grandma's house. There were some that were the same size as her, and all of them creeped her out, and here is one sitting on their deck.

"The outside trash, right?"

"Yes, the outside trash. I'm not bringing it in here. It might be infested with bugs," Peter answers Maggie. There ios no reason to mention that he feels just a little bit more than creeped out about the doll. Peter has never been a fan of dolls, and this one is especially creepy. He did not want it in the house.

Grabbing a plastic shopping bag, Peter steps outside and scoops the doll into the bag, and carries it to the trash can that is along the side of their house. It is one of those big grey barrels of a trash can with a lid on it. There are already a couple trash bags in the can. They have been getting rid of packing supplies.

While Peter would never admit it to Maggie, the doll so disturbs him that he buries it under another trash bag, making it unlikely that anyone would dig it out or that it would climb out on its own. Not that dolls could really come to life and move under their own power. That is a Hollywood trick only, or so he tells himself.

The next morning, it is River who let them know that something is not quite right. River has been enjoying her backyard since they moved in. Not once, not even in the heaviest rainstorm, has River not wanted to go outside, until that morning. This morning she refuses to go near the back door and whines when Maggie moves to let her outside. The doll is back, and even River is concerned about it.

"I thought you got rid of it," Maggie whispers to Peter as she stares at the doll behind the safety of the screen door. Maggie does not actually think that the doll can hear her, but she also is not sure that the doll can not hear her. She is pretty certain that a doll could not remove itself from the trash, but yet, here it is, on their deck again.

"I thought I did, too," Peter answers, whispering as well. He is reluctant to step outside and touch the doll again, even though he knows that was what is going to have to happen. He knows that there is no chance that Maggie iss going to even approach the doll. He can almost smell her fear of the doll, if that makes any sense to anyone but him.The way that she stares at it, wide-eyed and intensely, is certainly a clear indicator of her discomfort around the toy.

"I say we burn it. We put it in the grill, and burn it. We'll buy new racks for the grill," Maggie is not messing around with this doll. The grill she is referring to is a charcoal grill. It is round and has a heavy lid. They would weigh down the lid and make sure the doll did not get out.

Maggie likes the idea of using fire to get rid of negative or evil things. Fire is cleasening, and not too many things came back after being burnt to a char. Although, if the doll did, Maggie is convinced that she would simply move away and let the doll have the house. Maybe Peter would stay and get the house exorised, and she and River would simply move into a hotel while that happened. That sounds like a good plan.

"Yes, that sounds like a plan," Peter agrees. He immediately goes and gets the charcoal and lighter fluid. This is happening now, at eight o'clock in the morning. The neighbors were going to think they were insane, but better that than be held hostage by a baby's toy.

Walking around the house so that he did not have to pass by the doll, Peter preps the grill, getting the flames high and the coals hot. He is very glad that he had decided to put the grill in the yard, and not on the deck like his original plan was. If it had been on the deck, he would have had to have passed close to the doll in order to reach the grill. Using tongs, he picks up the doll and throws it onto the grill.

It is either his imagination or the sound of the plastic melting that causes what sounds like a sob to occur. It is that same plastic melting that makes him swear that he hears someone say no, as he slams the lid down. He does not lift the lid at all to check on the condition of the doll. He just let it cook and melt for several hours. He figures by the time the coals burn down, the doll would be nothing more than a piece of plastic slag. The doll is not coming back this time.

The Mouse — 1975

Annie quickly settles into her new home. It is a quiet home, if not always peaceful. Mom works a lot of hours cleaning other people's homes, and Dad works even more hours at his foundry job. They always return home tired, often too tired to cook and clean, even if Teddy expected it of Kitty. That leaves a lot of hours for Annie to quietly read in her room. It also gives her time to help around the house.

To help her Mom, Annie would often do the best that she could to clean the house. She would sweep the floors and vacuum the carpets. She wipes down the counters and makes sure her toys are put away every day. Using a chair, she is able to reach the sink and does the dishes. She could not reach the washer though, so doing laundry was out of the question. She is a good child, and she loves to be helpful.

The house is old though, very old. It was just over sixty years old when the Koonz moved in. This meant that there were some problems that happen, no matter how clean the house is kept. There are always some centipedes and spiders that can be found running around the basement. Occasionally, there would be a bird that managed to find its way into the house. The biggest of these problems, though, are the mice. No matter how much Annie scrubs and cleans, she often found mouse poop behind the coffee maker and the toaster, on the counters, and sometimes on the window ledges. There was never mouse poop in any of the other rooms, just the kitchen. That is bad enough, though.

Annie never says anything to her parents, despite finding evidence of mice in the kitchen. She knows what her Dad would do. He would go to war against the mice, buying bait, glue traps, and snap traps. Annie was simply too soft-hearted to want to kill the mice for simply wanting somewhere warm to live, and maybe whatever food that they could happen to find. It was unfortunate for the mice that Teddy did see one, one night after he got home from work. What happens next was just as Annie predicted.

The next day the house is loaded with mice traps, poison, and glue traps. They are plastered everywhere that the mice might go and there is nothing Annie could do to stop it. She tries to argue with her Dad that it is not necessary, but he simply ignores her and goes on setting up every mouse killing method that he can come up with. Annie goes to her room and cries.

"Annie, honey, can I come in?" Kitty asks, lightly tapping on Annie's bedroom door.

"Sure," Annie answers, weakly and sadly. The tremble in her voice signals the tears that she had cried and the ones that she could soon be crying again.

Kitty opens the door and steps inside, closing it behind her. "Honey, have you been crying about the mice?" Kitty knows the answer. She always knows with her daughter.

"Yes," Annie may have let her Mom in her room, but that did not mean she is ready to look at her though. She keeps her eyes downcast to the floor. She wipes her tears with the back of her hand and sniffles. Crying always made her nose run and make her eyes red and puffy. Her cheeks are blotchy, as well. She looks as miserable as she is feeling.

"Do you know why we cannot have mice in the house?"

"Dad says it is because they are dirty. I overheard him talking to himself while he was setting the traps." Annie's lips began to tremble and tears began to fall from her eyes once again. It was just too much sadness for her little body to contain. She can just picture the mice, scared and hurt, running away from the traps. Some of them would even die, and that might be the mommy mouse or a baby mouse, and that is too much sorrow for her.

"That's true. If the mice were allowed to run around the house, they could get us very sick. They poop everywhere, and pee constantly. Plus they carry diseases, like rabies. People do not recover from rabies. If one were to have rabies and bite you, you could get infected and die. You might not even notice that you had gotten bit until it was too late," Kitty reaches to her daughter, pulling her close and holding her tightly.

"Your Dad is doing what he has to do to protect this family. He does not want to kill the mice, but he does not have much of a choice." Kitty is not sure that was true, but voicing that doubt would not help Annie, so she kept it to herself. Teddy did seem to enjoy setting the traps just a little bit too much. It is almost as though he was not thinking about how much pain might be caused by the traps, but rather on simply eliminating an enemy, even if it is just a tiny rodent.

"But I like the mice. They're cute." Embraced in her mother's arms, Annie begins to calm down a bit. Annie is just a little child, that much emotion takes a big toll on her. Now, after grieving and being angry, she is ready to bargain for the mice's lives. She begins to hiccup a little as she stopped sobbing. The hiccups shake her entire body as they strike every couple of breathes. They make Annie appear even younger than she is.

"Oh, I know they're cute. But they are still dirty. They cannot stay in the house." There was to be no stay of execution for the mice. Not even Kitty could be persuaded to live and let live when it came to the mice. Her voice is cold and has the ring of finality. Annie knows better than to argue with that tone. She would do nothing but lose.

***

It is as Annie is cleaning one day, that she sees a mouse caught in the glue trap and could not stand for it anymore. Grabbing the glue trap, mouse, and all, she devises a plan. She is saving at least this mouse keeping him as a pet. She already has everything that she needs, and while saving one mouse is not going to change the world, for this one mouse, it would. This one mouse, at least, would be allowed to live.

The first step is to free the mouse from the trap. For this, she uses warm water and soap. It is almost as if the mouse knows what she was doing because he holds perfectly still while she works. Annie knew that he might be so still because he was terrified, but she wants to believe it was because he understood, so she does. She speaks quietly to him, explaining every action as though he might understand what she is saying. Surprisingly, the mouse did not bite

Annie while she works, even though he had every opprotunity. She is not sure what she would do if he had bites her. He might have rabies, but if he bites her and she gets rabies, there is nothing that anyone could do anyway, so she would just keep quiet about it. She did not want to get the mouse in trouble, if he bites her.

Once she is done, she holds the mouse in a loose grip, now clean of the glue. She sets him in a cardboard box that she kept stationary in while she goes to get him some bread to eat. She is so pleased when he decides to stay in the box rather than escape. He looks cute and almost cuddly, standing in the corner of the box. His grey fur, soft and clean after his bath. She was even more pleased when he begins to eat the bread and drink the water that she put in a small soda cap for him. He is going to make it. She saved his life and now she has a pet all of her own.

She keeps that mouse for a week. She builds him a little chair and table out of her legos. She feeds him whatever scraps she can find, and does her best to keep his soda cap filled with water. She checks on him every morning before school, and every afternoon after school. Annie has always wanted a pet, and now she has one, even if she has to keep him a secret from her parents. She thinks she is going to get away with keeping this one mouse, even though the war on his brethren was ongoing.

One day her father came home early from work. There had been a power out at the forge and the workers had been dismissed early. As he passes by Annie's room, he hears a light scratching coming from the room. Slowly, he opens the door, expecting to find a burglar. Instead, he is greeted with a clean and organized room. The bed is made and a stationary box is on top of it. The scratching noise is coming from the box.

Slowly, knowing what he will find in the box, Teddy walks over to the bed. Even more slowly, Teddy picks up the box, noting the pretty pink flowers that decorate the outside of the box. He remembers buying it for Annie last summer. She spent that summer and fall writing letters to her classmates. He is very sure that the box does not hold letters anymore. When he feels movement in the box, he almost drops it, but instead tightens his grip and forces himself to open the box.

A cold fury steals over Teddy Koonz when he sees the mouse that his daughter had been keeping in her room. Closing the lid of the box he makes the decision to teach her a lesson. Holding the lid closed, he shakes the box, hard. He keeps shaking the box for several minutes. He hears the little mouse's body break, but he does not stop shaking the box. Eventually his rage relaxes and then he sets the closed box back on the bed where he found it. He knows that Annie will rush up to her room and check on the mouse as soon as she gets home from school. Her lesson will be harsh, but necessary.

The sobs that come from Annie's chest almost makes Teddy regret his decision. He could not rightly say what had come over him to kill her pet mouse. Her secret pet mouse. He is almost ashamed, but at the same time, he is angry that she would keep something from him, her father. Her heartbreak breaks his heart, but she needs to learn who is in charge, and it is not her. He would be nice, and help her bury the mouse, box, legos, and all.

With great ceremony, Teddy leads Annie to the backyard. There, she stands by the raspberry bushes, while he digs a hole in the yard. Once it is big enough, he lets her set the box in the hole, and he covers it with the same dirt that he just dug up. He spreads the excess around the yard, making sure that there were no mounds of dirt to create a mud puddle later. He hopes that it will help her move on from her grief over such a stupid thing, the pet mouse. Annie never stops crying through the whole thing, and refuses dinner, preferring to go to bed hungry. Her sorrow is all consuming, at the moment.

The Lego — 2007

Maggie is walking barefoot in the dining room when she steps on something hard and sharp. Whatever it is, it digs itself deep into her foot, sticking there for a moment before falling off and onto the floor behind her, making a soft "ting" sound as it bounces off the hardwood floor.

Maggie is certain it was one of River's many bone toys, but River is usually very good at putting her toys away. It is not like her to leave a toy out. She may have just missed picking up a bone shard. No one could fault the dog for not getting everything when she cleaned up her toys. Maggie is just not so sure how she managed to miss it when she swept that morning. One of life's many mysteries when you live with a dog.

Turning around, Maggie bends down to pick up the offending object. It is a Lego. In particular, it is a grey, four-posted Lego. This asks far more questions than it answers. Hopefully, Peter would have those answers because this house was getting creepy with all the random things just appearing. The doll was only a few weeks ago, and that was terrifying.

"Honey, do you have any Legos?" Maggie is pretty certain that Peter does not own any legos, but if he did, then that would make for a much easier answer. It would make for a less concerning answer, anyway. Peter is sitting in the living room, watching television.

"Legos? You mean, like the building blocks?" Peter seems confused by the question, and Maggie's heart began to sink. This was not going to be an easily answered puzzle, after all. Peter turns to Maggie and pauses his television show. He likes to give her his full attention.

"Yeah, like the building blocks."

"Nope. Why?"

"Well, I found this Lego in the middle of the dining room floor. I found it by stepping on it," Maggie answers Peter and hands him the offending Lego.

Peter takes the block, holding it in the palm of his hand and looks at it with interest. "You found this on the dining room floor?"

"Yep," Maggie answers as she takes it back from Peter's outstretched hand.

"River must have found it outside and brought it in. She most likely decided to clean up the backyard. You know how she is, every little thing has to be picked up and put away. We trained her too well," Peter reasons. He is about to turn back to the television when Maggie continues.

"You really think so?"

"Do you remember when she was a year old, and we let her stay with my brother while we were out of town? What was the first thing she did?" Peter askes. He sighes as he speaks. He is exasperated and he really wants to watch his television show. Maggie is the priority though, not the television.

"She peed on his bed," Maggie laughs. Peter even laughs, remembering how proud she seemed to be to do that to his little brother. River's little nose was pointed to his ceiling while she peed, letting him know that this was now her bed. Paul, Peter's brother, handled it better than Peter would have. Instead of getting mad, he simply gathered the blankets and threw them in the wash before it could soak into his bed. That was what had convinced Maggie to let him watch her beloved little puppy.

"What was the other thing she did? After she peed on his bed." Peter asks once he is done laughing. It would not be funny if she did that to their bed, but his little brother's bed was hilarious.

"She went around his apartment and picked up every small object she could find and brought it to me. I had quite the little pile going on before we left," Maggie's eyes went a little distant, remembering how River was even more proud to have found all these small things at Paul's house.

River likes to help clean up around the house. Every time Maggie or Peter would ask her, "How many toys do you have out?" she will promptly get to work, picking up her toys and putting them in the toy box. She learned the trick quite by accident. Maggie would always say that phrase right before she began to gather River's toys. River simply mimicked her Mom, learning how to clean house in the process.

"Exactly. She probably found this outside and wanted to bring it to one of us, and dropped it. I wouldn't worry about it, too much," Peter reasons, finally able to turn back to his television show.

Walking into the kitchen, Maggie put the mystery aside. It was most likely something that River picked up. That definitely makes more sense than the idea that there is a ghost leaving Legos around the house. Smiling and laughing at her own silliness, she almost misses the small mouse pellets that dotted their way along the counters.

"Peter, we have a mouse!" Maggie shouts to the living room as she ducks under the kitchen sink. There she finds and pulls out a small black box. It has an open tube, a spot for bait, and an on/off switch. It is an electric mousetrap.

"Set the trap," Peter calls back.

"I am. I just wanted you to know," Maggie answers while filling the bait part of the trap with a smear of peanut butter and checking the battery. With a buzz and a flash of green light, the trap is set. The next morning, the light is flashing red, and the mouse is dead.

***

It is later that month that Peter finds a Lego on the dining room floor. He did not step on it as his wife did. Instead, he notices it as he is walking through the room because it is bright red and a two-posted block.

"River brought in another Lego and left it in the dining room," Peter mentions to Maggie when she steps into the living room with his dinner after a long day at work. Maggie likes to cook him dinner and bring it into him. He told her over and over again that he could get his own food, or at least dish his own food, and to serve herself first. She would smile and ignore him, serving him dinner first and herself second.

"Another one? Weird," Maggie answers him.

It only got weirder for the couple when the next morning, they find their electric trap flashing red once again. Another mouse has met its end. The building blocks and the mouse almost appear to be related in some manner.

"That is super weird. River finds a Lego, and then a mouse appears. If I were superstitious, I would almost believe that the two events are linked," Maggie says as she emptied the trap into the outside trash container. Peter had gotten the first one, so it was her turn this time.

"You are superstitious," Peter answers. "The difference is that we both know that there is no way that the mouse and the lego can possibly be related. None. Remember the quote from Ian Fleming, 'Once is happenstance. Twice is coincidence. Three times is enemy action.' I am not going to worry about it until we find a third mouse and a third Lego," Peter answers with certainty. Maggie was just being her normal nervous self. This is nothing, and he knows it. Paranormal activity only exists in books and movies.

Later that evening, when Peter finds the third Lego and the third flashing light, he does not tell Maggie. He simply stands there, holding the Lego, watching the light flash. He knows that she would suggest it might be some type of spirit trying to communicate with them. He is no longer certain she is wrong. Burying the Lego in the trash, he empties the mouse trap. He would not tell her about this. He never did tell her about it, even when the truth became apparent.

Dad's Bad Day — 1975

Teddy Koonz works Monday through Saturday, from six in the morning to six in the evening. It is back-breaking work. It is hot work. He works at a forge, hammering molten steel into bars. It is exhausting work. At times, the wages do not seem to make the work worth it. He does it because he knows how to do it, and to quit is to take the roof from over Kitty and Annie's heads.

Swinging a hammer every day takes a toll on Teddy's body. His joints creak when he stands up. His back hurts him nearly constantly. His feet are callused over, giving him soles thicker than most shoes had. It also gives him the type of strength you only got out of people who work for a living. Every part of him is cut and well-built. He has to be careful when working around smaller people. It is easy to forget how strong he is.

It is a hot summer day. Teddy's back has been bothering him more than ever, lately. He has not been sleeping well, the house is just too hot. He looked into getting a window unit air conditioner, but they are just too expensive. If he made more at the foundry, if Kitty made more cleaning houses, if having a daughter was not so expensive, if...

With every swing of the hammer, Teddy can feel himself lose a little bit more of his control. He feels like lashing out at someone, anyone. If he did not share this pain with someone, it was going to tear him apart from the inside out. As he slammed his hammer down, sparks rained. As his partner drove his hammer down, some of those sparks brushed Teddy, lighting his temper and giving him a target.

"RON! Can't you watch where you are hitting, you fucking idiot!" Teddy knows that Ron did not intend for sparks to land on him. Teddy knows that Ron does not have any real control on how the sparks landed. Instead, all of that was dependent on everything from a piece of metal stuck to the hammer to how the wind blew through the open bay doors. It did not matter at that moment though. The fight is all that matters.

Ron is a big man in his own right. You have to be if you are going to swing a fifty-pound hammer. "Fuck off, Teddy. You know full well that the sparks go where they go. I've been burned half a dozen times today, so far, and you don't hear me bitching. If you can't take the heat, either wear kevlar, or get out of the forge." His blue eyes are flashing, angry. He does not dislike Teddy, but sometimes Teddy can be a bit of a bully, and Ron is not interested in being a punching bag.

"Fuck you!" Teddy screams as he throws down his hammer, charging at Ron. Swinging on Ron, Teddy never realized that Ron never dropped his hammer. Instead, he takes a hard blow to the ribs with that fifty-pound hammer Ron wields with practiced ease.

Ron had seen Teddy coming. Figuring that he did not want to get into a prolonged fight with the man, he decides to end the fight quickly. A quick jab to the man's sternum with the head of the hammer was all that it took to drive the breath and the rage from Teddy Koonz. Ron did not even put much force into the hit, relying upon the weight of the hammer to do the job. It is most effective.

The fight, despite how quickly it was over, drew the attention of the supervisor, Mr. Freer. "What the hell happened here?" He demands of Ron, grabbing him by the shoulder and stepping between Teddy, who was still on the floor, and Ron, who stands over him.

"Just a little misunderstanding between Teddy and me, here. Nothing to get too worked up about," Ron downplays the scene. He even throws in a stray smile and an "aw shucks" shuffle of his feet. What was done was done. No sense in getting either of them fired by making it out to be what it was, Teddy attacking Ron out of temper. It was doubtful that Teddy was going to be stupid enough to try to go after Ron a second time.

"Right, a misunderstanding. Between you, the most laid-back person in this whole building, and Teddy, the hothead. Right. Who saw it happen?" Mr. Freer gives Ron's shoulder a slight shove back, making more room between the two men. He looks around, searching for witnesses. No one steps forward. No one wanted to cross Teddy. Once he is gone, then they will freely talk about how much he bothered them and how uncomfortable he made them feel. For now, they stand in silence.

"Teddy, get yourself up and meet me in the office. Ron, you too," Mr. Freer orders as he scowls at the men surrounding him. "The rest of you, if you have something to say, say it. If not, get yourselves back to work." He knows them for the cowards they are, waiting for someone else to make the first move before they make one themselves, even if everyone would benefit.

***

Up in the office, it is still hot, but not as hot as it is next to the molten steel. The chairs are the type of filthy that can not be cleaned, but it did not matter to the two men sitting in them. They were already filthy from sweat and the steel. A little more dirt was hardly anything to worry about. They watch as Mr. Freer runs the security film of what happened on the floor just a few minutes ago. They know what it will show.

"I do not want to hear an excuse. I don't care who said what. What I care about is who struck first. That could not be clearer. Teddy, you have been warned that if you could not control your temper, you could not work here. Get your shit and get the fuck out of my foundry. I will have a couple of guys escort you, but I am sure you will not give them any problems, right?

"Ron, you are suspended for three days. You will finish out today, and then not come back until next week. I don't want to see hide nor hair of you before that. You understand?" The last line was hardly a question. This was not a debate, this was judgment.

Mr. Freer did not want to punish Ron, but he was relieved to get rid of Teddy. He had been a trouble employee since he started there. If anyone else had spoken up, he could have prevented this whole thing simply by getting rid of Teddy months ago, but no one wanted to talk. Instead he had to wait until something like this happened. Now it has, and now his shop would be just a little bit better without the trouble spot in it.

***

Kitty comes home, exhausted but glad to be done with her day. She cleaned four houses that day, and it made for a long day. Her back is bothering her, and her feet hurt. Now she is home and had to get dinner ready before Teddy got home. Plus there is Annie to see to, that young girl most likely has something she wants to show her as soon as she walks in the door. Annie is always eager to see her like that.

She knew it was going to be bad when she walked in, and Teddy was already drunk on the sofa. Poor Annie sits crouched in front of the fireplace, quietly holding Dolly. At least she does not look like she had any bruises on her. Being scared is okay, but being hurt is something else. Kitty could almost forgive him scaring her.

With there being nothing else she can do, Kitty walks into the kitchen and starts making dinner. Teddy could tell her what happened when he sobered up.

The Rocking Chair — 2007

"Look at these adorable rocking chairs!" Maggie and Peter are out, doing some yard sailing. It is a nice change from staying inside to watching television. Not much beats retail therapy coupled with a walk outside, in the bright summer sun. The weather is warm enough not to need jackets or hoodies, but cool enough to be refreshing. Throw in a couple of drinks, and it could almost be a party.

Buying rocking chairs was not on Peter's list of things that they might buy though. Rocking chairs are big and heavy. He would need to go back and get the car for those. He was expecting books and knick-knacks. He has a cart just for those types of things, instead, Maggie is pointing out a rocking chair.

"What are you going to do with a rocking chair?" Peter asks. Reasoning with Maggie has never been an effective form of persuasion, but maybe just once it would work. Yeah, and maybe pigs would learn to fly. He hopes that some researcher somewhere is working on that problem, a lot of people would have a lot of interesting promises to keep when he succeeds in making pigs fly.

"Sit in it, obviously," Maggie answers, smiling down at the rocking chair. It is a nice rocking chair. It has the traditional curved rockers on the bottom and a red cushion on the seat. The wood is intricately engraved. It has a sense of value, of weight, of importance. It is an imposing rocking chair. It is bound to be a heavy chair. Just looking at it makes Peter's back and knees sore.

Maggie drops down on it and begins to rock gently. Peter knows he has lost the battle to avoid buying the chair well before it even began. "Fine, we'll get the rocking chair. How much is it?"

Maggie begins looking around herself, first looking over one shoulder and then the next, trying to find the price tag while still seated in the rocking chair. Peter walks around it, but he does not see it. Finally, Maggie stands up and finds the price tag that was on the seat. It is a small piece of masking tape with the number $25, on it. "Twenty-five dollars," Maggie announces, smiling proudly. "I am pretty sure I can get it down to twenty," she says in a much quieter voice, almost conspiratorially.

Peter has never been comfortable watching his wife haggle. She thinks of it as an art form. He does not think saving a couple of dollars is worth the hassle. "No, it is worth twenty-five dollars. We'll pay the man, and I'll start walking back to go get the car."

Watching the transaction go smoothly between the hard-faced woman who was selling the rocking chair, and his joyful wife, Peter turns to walk the mile back to the car. Maggie would stay close to the sale and make sure that no one else tries to take her rocking chair. Plus with Maggie still at the house where she bought the chair, he would be able to find the right yard sale faster than if he had to drive around, looking for addresses and trying to remember what the house looked like.

***

Peter is not slow making his way back to the car. He is not distracted by other locations, stops, or even cute dogs. He is gone for a total of maybe twenty minutes. In those twenty minutes, Maggie also picked up a child-sized version of the rocking chair she bought with him, a large house plant, and a sign for the front door. He knew better than to leave her alone. He did it anyway, and he got what he expected, more stuff.

With a sigh, he flattens the seats in the car, giving them as much room as possible to load the stuff in. Even then, the house plant has to ride in the front with Maggie. She set the wicker basket with the large peace lily right between her feet, playing with the leaves as he drives away from the sale.

He could be upset, spending so recklessly on things they did not need. They did not even have children. They could not have children. Who was the child-sized rocking chair for? But, the look on Maggie's face is one of pure joy. She is proud of what she got, so he would not ruin it for her. He does have to know though, "Who is the little rocking chair for?"

"My siblings all have children. I'm planning on setting the rocking chairs under the light by the fireplace. I can sit in one and read, and they can sit in one. It will be perfect!" Ah, the explanation makes a kind of sense. Except he is pretty sure that if the kids came over, they would be far more interested in movies and River than the books. He was not about that break that bubble though. Maybe she was right.

***

The area by the fireplace had been empty so far. They call it the dining room, but they do not have a dining room table to put there. Instead, a couple of end tables sit under the windows, and a long television stand is set up as a table between them. There are a few pictures on the walls, but other than that, it was empty.

Peter had to admit that it looks a lot more inviting with two rocking chairs and a small table sitting in front of the fireplace. The house plant, one that they discovered was called a Peace Lily, sits to the right of the fireplace. It almost looked like a scene out of a magazine.

Grabbing a book, Maggie sits down in her rocking chair and begins to slowly rock while reading. Peter grabs a small afghan, one that Maggie's mother made her, and tucks it around Maggie. He then makes her a cup of coffee and settles down for the night. He liked taking care of his wife. She looks very comfortable and happy, sitting in a rocking chair, rocking quietly and reading a book. Even River looks content to watch her.

Coming back into the dining room, well, he guesses they can now call it a sitting room, he carefully balances the cup between his two hands. In addition to coffee, he has put a healthy amount of cream in it. Then there are the marshmallow and the sprinkles he added. He had seen her do it once and thought it was adorable. Now every time he makes her coffee, he goes to the extreme with it. Her smile is worth it.

Looking up from the coffee, he stops, almost dropping the cup in his shock. "Maggie, look at the other rocking chair," he murmurs, not wanting to scare Maggie.

Maggie looks up at Peter's suggestion and turns pale as she watches the small rocking chair to her right go back and forth of its own accord. Someone or something was rocking in the chair. They are moving it with enough force that the rocking chair is moving towards the wall. It was only once it struck the wall that the rocking stops.

"Tell me again that we don't have a ghost," Maggie demands in a shocked voice.

"There must have been a draft or something. Ghosts do not exist," Peter sounds far less sure this time than he has any other time. This event was rather hard to dismiss..

"A draft that neither of us felt and did not even move the plant leaves," Maggie answers back a little bit harsher than she has intended. She could not believe that Peter still refuses to believe in ghosts. The evidence can not be clearer.

"I really don't know what to say, Maggie. I don't understand it," Peter responds, setting the coffee cup next to her, and then retreating to the living room to watch television and forget what he just saw.

Happy Birthday — 1975

It is August 8th. To the average person, it is just an average Friday. To Annie, it is her ninth birthday. She has made it another year, and today they would celebrate that fact. Annie is certain that her parents would buy her a cake, presents, and maybe even a puppy. Annie has always wanted a puppy. Annie did not bring it up though, Mom said no puppies, and her mouse had died. Maybe pets were not in her future.

Since it is summer, Annie is determined to spend the morning outside, out of her parents' way. Mom is home, working in the house. Dad has not been to work in a while, but Annie is sure it was okay. Dad has lost his job before and they always call him back, or he goes somewhere else. This time would be no different.

Mom says the money was tight, but Annie really could not remember a time when her Mom did not say that. There always seems to be something to eat and Dad always has a beer, so money could not be too tight. Annie has heard of people in other countries that did not even have clean water to drink, let alone food to eat. Annie has a hard time imagining that, but then she saw the commercials and could not understand it. Surely, they have homes and kitchen faucets with running water. Why would they choose to drink dirty water?

Even if there are no presents, Annie is certain there would be at least cake. Mom has never forgotten about her birthday and always makes her a cake. Annie likes cake, especially the chocolate kind. One time Mom made a chocolate cake and put strawberries between the layers and on the top. It was the best cake ever. Annie is hoping to get the same type of cake this year. A girl is only nine once, so it is a special day.

So far neither of her parents have mentioned her birthday. That does not matter though, she knows in her heart of hearts that there is no way her parents would forget it. Instead, she would show them that she is a big girl, and not make a fuss about them possibly forgetting her birthday. She is a big girl, almost double digits, practically an adult. She can be patient.

The morning wore on, and lunch came and went without acknowledgment of Annie's birthday. They all sit around the kitchen table, eating baloney sandwiches on white bread. Annie likes baloney sandwiches, so she is okay with having those for lunch. She does wish that there were some cookies to have as a treat after lunch, but no sense in wishes. Instead, grabbing a cola out of the refrigerator, she goes up to her room to read some.

Annie does not own a lot of books. She loves books, but books are expensive and the library is free. There is a large library eight blocks away. It is a huge square building with marble floors. The stairs are well worn with age, and the railings are dark with the thousands of hands that have glided along them. Every time Annie walks into the library, she feels like she was walking into a castle full of books.

It was those books that made the library even more impressive. There are what seems like millions of books in the library. The shelves are heavy with books. The shelves are bowed under the weight of the books. They line the walls, leaving the center space open. That center space is a cut-out so you can see the floors below. Annie loves to spend her days, when her parents are both at work, at the library, reading.

Since both of her parents are home, Annie is home as well. They would insist on going with her to the library, and neither of her parents are interested in just sitting and reading like she is., although her Mom could do her handwork there. They would get bored and want to leave within a couple of hours, just as she is getting started with her literary adventures. Instead, she spends the afternoon sitting on her bed, in front of the window, reading her favorite novel, Black Beauty.

Annie always dreams about owning her very own horse. It did not have to look like Black Beauty, just be a nice horse that she could ride and spend time with. She could picture herself laying along the back of her horse, reading books while it munched on clovers. Annie was not sure where she would keep a horse, but she was sure that she could figure out something if she ever had the opportunity to own one.

Annie slipped off to a short nap before dinner, waking when her mom lightly taps on her door. Her mom motions her to be quiet as they descend the steps down the stairs and into the kitchen. Mom keeps her finger pressed to her lips as they sit themselves down at the table to eat.

Dinner is a quiet affair. Dad is drunk and passed out on the sofa. Mom is tired and upset. Annie is all but forgotten about. Mom makes some chicken nuggets in the oven and some macaroni and cheese on the stove. Annie has to have milk with her meal, not soda. That is the rule, and there are no exceptions.

After they ate, Annie and Kitty left their plates on the table and went out the back door and into the backyard. "Happy birthday, baby," Kitty whispers to Annie. Her sadness tints the words, allowing Annie to feel the disappointment that Kitty has in herself for not being able to provide Annie the birthday that Kitty feels Annie deserves.

"Thanks, Mom. I'm nine now," Annie answers her in just as quiet of a voice. Her whisper does not carry the note of recrimination that Kitty expects. Neither of them want to risk waking Teddy.

"I know. You're my big girl, growing up so fast. I know I always make a cake. With your dad out of work though, eggs are just too expensive. I'm sorry. As soon as I can, I will make you an extra special cake, with strawberries and blueberries," Kitty explains, wiping her tears from her cheek with the back of her hand. Kitty is not afraid to cry in front of her daughter.

Annie is not really surprised that there was no cake. She has been home all day. She would have noticed if the house began to smell like baking. She is still sad to know that this year, her ninth birthday, there would be no cake and no presents. She is not even sure that her dad remembered her birthday. At least her Mom acknowledged it.

"That's okay. I don't need cake. I have you," Annie answers her mom, hugging her. She pretends not to mind her mother's tears in her hair.

What's this? Cake? — 2007

"Wednesday birthdays are the worse!" Maggie explains, not that anyone would argue against her on that point. "You have to go to work. It is not even worth it to take a day off at either end of the week because your birthday is in the dead center of the work week."

Peter and she are walking into the house on the Saturday before Peter's 38th birthday, August 4th. It is one o' clock in the morning. They are just coming back from listening to music at their favorite bar. Listening to music, dancing, and having one too many drinks. They are lucky to make it home in one piece, sometimes.

"No, Wednesday birthdays are the best. Because it is in the dead center of the week, I can claim both weekends as my birthday weekend. And I will. This is my birthday weekend, and next weekend is my birthday weekend. We shall party like we are a decade younger than we are," He answers with a laugh. Peter might have a good point there. Both he and Maggie may have a bit more to drink than recommended. But they had been having fun.

They went out to one of their favorite outside bars and listened to music. They were not expecting to meet up with any of their friends, but they managed to end up in the center of a whole party of their friends. What started out as a drink, turned into more than a few. Good thing for taxis, although they were going to have to walk back to the bar in the morning to pick up their car.

"You're gonna claim two weekends as your birthday weekend? Next, you're gonna say that this whole week is your birthday week," Maggie teases as they practically fall through the door.

"Absolutely. That means you have to do anything I ask," Peter murmurs as he playfully grabs Maggie's shoulders, pulling her close.

Looking up at him with fake innocent eyes, Maggie whispers, "Anything?"

Peter's eyes are devious as he smiles down at her, "Anything."

"Hum... that sounds like fun," Maggie smiles back at him, eyes twinkling. She then spins and takes off through the downstairs rooms, and towards the stairs, barely making it onto the first steps before Peter playfully catches her again.

***

The next morning is bright and brought reality crashing down on the couple. They are no longer in their early twenties. Hangovers are real, and they still have to get the car. Taking their showers and having toast for breakfast, they decide that getting the car is a family affair. Grabbing River's harness and lead, they all troupe out the front door and walk to pick up the car.

"So, it's been a while since we've seen any ghost activity," Maggie mentions as they walk. It had been almost a full month without any ghost activity that Maggie noticed. She knew that Peter would not want to talk about it, but they have two miles to walk. When you have almost two miles to go, conversation seems to be a given.

"I am still not convinced we had any ghost activity. The rocking chair could easily have moved due to a draft through the ventilation system," Peter is admitting to nothing. He has always been a skeptic, and he will continue to be a skeptic.

"A draft that neither of us felt?"

"A very localized draft, yes." Peter and Maggie walk in silence with River between them for a couple more blocks before Peter speaks up again. "Have you ever experienced ghost behavior before this house?"

"Yep. There was a ghost in the house that I lived in as a child. Then there was the ghost at work. The one at my parents' home was creepy. He'd stalk up and down the stairs at all hours of the night and stare into our bedrooms. But he never interacted with us. I am pretty sure my sisters saw him, but I don't think my brother or parents did.

"The ghost at work is different. I never saw him, but he would move things.

One time he moved the caps I was working on while I was setting them up for inspection. When I moved them back, he did it again. Freaked out, I went and got Johnny, one of the techs, and made him watch me put everything back. And the ghost moved them all a third time. What's that called, oh yeah, enemy action. Johnny said it was static electricity, but you could just tell he did not believe that." Maggie relates her experiences without fear. Instead, she sounds almost curious about the events she was talking about, as though she wishes she knew more about them. Maybe they could get ahold of a paranormal group in town and have their house investigated.

"Did you ever figure out who those ghosts were?" Peter askes, interrupting Maggie's thoughts about how one goes about getting their house investigated.

"No idea about who the one at my parents' home is. The one at work is an old employee who had a heart attack there. I don't know his name though."

"I'm pretty sure we don't have a ghost, but it might be worthwhile to check into the history of our house. Besides, it could be fun," Peter suggests. Who knows, it might even get Maggie to drop the idea of the house being haunted, and find a new hobby, investigative researching, or something like that.

Maggie and Peter dropped the topic of the ghost like it was a hot potato, instead, they start to talk about updates that they would like to do to the house. They talk about the new doors, new windows, and new plants for the front of the house. There are so many options that the two miles to pick up the car pass without anyone noticing.

After such a walk, everyone is tired. Rather than turning around and heading right back home, they decide to swing by the local Dairy Queen. Two ice cream cones and a pup cup later, everyone is refreshed and feeling good. Today is a good day.

***

Wednesday, despite being Peter's actual birthday, was a pretty typical day for the couple, right up until they get home from work. There, sitting on the back steps is a birthday cake. It was not a full cake, just a single, perfectly cut, square piece of cake. It sat on the dead center of a small paper plate. It is vanilla, with a white frosting and brightly colored sprinkles. There is a candle stuck into it. At least the candle is not lit, that would have been too much. It brought the two of them to a complete standstill, unable to pass the cake.

"There is birthday cake on the stairs," Maggie whispers to Peter, not taking her eyes off the cake.

"I take it that you did not put it there?" Peter whispers back. He, too, is watching the cake like it might preform tricks or something.

"Nope. And now I am convinced that someone or something is in our house. I've seen documentaries where you find strangers living in the crawl spaces and hollow parts of the walls in old homes like these."

"I am sure that a neighbor or someone had a birthday, and sat on our steps to enjoy their cake. Then River probably barked and scared them away, leaving their cake. It's not a ghost. And there is no one else living in our house besides us. There is not enough room in the house for that," Peter reasons.

"Are you going to keep the cake? It was probably given to you by the ghost for your birthday," Maggie teases, trying to break the tension that they both are feeling and the sense of anxiety that is building in her. It does not work. They are both just as nervous as they were the moment before that.

"Um, no. I don't think I'm going to eat the cake, no matter who made it," Peter laughs as he scoops up the plate and carries it inside. River thrusts her nose up towards the cake that Peter is carrying. She is certain that the cake belongs to her. It is unfortunate for her that Peter and Maggie are simply too paranoid for her health to allow her to eat the cake that they found on their back steps. It could be poised. Instead, Peter disposes of it in the trash like a civilized person. Although if a second piece appears, he will be burning that one like he burnt the doll.

The Electricity — 1975

Teddy spends the next couple of months at home, drinking, rather than looking for a job. Getting fired from the foundry has thrown him for a loop. He had been fired from jobs before. He was fired from a couple of them for drinking on the job. One for attendance, and now this one for fighting. He really did expect them to call him back. He is beginning to think that the problem is not the supervisors or the other employees, but him, and he does not know how to handle that.

Kitty's house cleaning job is good for extra cash, but it does not pay enough to make ends meet. She has been picking up every extra available shift, working almost every day for twelve hours a day on most days. Then she is expected to come home and make dinner, clean the dishes and kitchen, and get Annie ready for bed, all while smiling. It is getting too much for her to do. The stress is building, and it is building fast.

The first utility to be turned off is the phone. Kitty and Teddy have been behind on the phone bill for a while. It is always the last bill that they pay since it does not seem that important to them whether the phone works or not. The only phone calls they ever get are from either Kitty's job or bill collectors. While it is annoying to miss potential work shifts by not having a phone, it is nice to be able to enjoy a dinner without a bill collector calling.

Then the cable is shut off. This caused no end of raging from Teddy. He likes to watch his sports on the television, and he needs cable to be able to do that. The local channels do not come in well with the rabbit ears and they only had local sports. Rather than getting a job to get cable turned back on, he takes to going to the corner bar to watch his sports.

That is okay with Annie. That means that she can leave and go to the library on her bike. She has never cared to watch television, although some of the cartoons are nice on Saturday mornings before Dad wakes up. Instead, she would rather read, so packing her book bag, she hops on her bike and rides to the library after Dad leaves to go to the bar. She just has to make sure that she is back before either of her parents comes home, otherwise, she would have to explain where she has been. She does not want them to ban her from going to the library.

It is a problem when the electricity is shut off. Everything in the house except the water heater is run off electricity. Without electricity, they can not cook their food. They can not keep their refrigerator cold. They can not turn on a single light. They at least could heat the house. They still have a gas fireplace.

Annie discovers the power is off after she comes back from the library. She had not clicked on any of the lights downstairs, but since it was an overcast day, she decides she would use her bedside lamp to read. When she clicked it on, it did not turn on. Assuming the light is out, she goes downstairs to get a fresh bulb. She has to turn on the kitchen light to see into the cabinets where the bulbs are stored, but that does not come on either. She glances over to the oven clock, and that is out. That's when she knows they have no power.

Annie stays up in her room when Teddy comes home. She knew that he would go into the kitchen and grab a beer from the refrigerator. She does not want to be in his sight when he realizes that the power is out and his beer is warm. She has nothing at all to do with the power being off, but she still does not want to be blamed for it. She sits up in her room, reading by the hazy light outside until it gets too dark to see. By then, Kitty had come home.

"We ain't got no power!" Teddy bellows as soon as Kitty walks in the door.

"Um, okay. Do the neighbors have power? Maybe there is a blockwide power out," Kitty suggests. She has not even had a chance to take her coat off or set down her purse.

Teddy lungs for her, grabbing her by the back of her neck, half dragging her to the front windows. Kitty drops her purse, pens, and papers going everywhere. Her wallet clatters to the floor, along with the coins she uses to ride the bus to and from her workplace.

"Does it look like there is a block-wide power out?" Teddy screams as he forces her to look at homes that are brightly lit. Theirs is the only home that is dark on the block.

"No. Teddy, you're hurting me," Kitty cries out. She expects him to let her go, to apologize for hurting her. Instead, he throws her backward, away from the windows. She hits the couch, hard, pushing it back, scratching the hardwood flooring. She gasps as she lands, the wind has been knocked out of her.

"Where is the money that was supposed to go to pay the bills? Huh, bitch?" Teddy screams. He is towering over Kitty, ready to strike.

"You drank it!" Kitty spits back at him. She knows what is coming next. She is not afraid. She is angry. She is the only one trying to make this work. She is the one working. She does all the work in the house, too. Yet, Teddy stands above her, ready to blame her for his problems, his failings. Too bad righteous anger makes poor armor.

"Bullshit!" Teddy screams as he swings his leg, lashing out to kick at Kitty. He is drunk and misses as much as he hits, but it is more than enough. Kitty has done what she can to protect her face, but her back is black and blue by the time he is done, even though her coat. It hurt to take a deep breath. She just lays there, beaten, long after he goes upstairs to bed. She is just relieved that Annie did not see this. It would have been too much for Kitty to bear. Annie might not have seen it, but she did hear it.

The Lights — 2007

"Honey! Could you bring up a light bulb?" Maggie calls down the stairs. She had gone to turn on the bedroom light but had gotten nothing. The hallway light is on, so it is not a power outage, it is just the one light. They have a box of bulbs in the kitchen cabinet just in case a bulb burnt out.

"Sure," Peter yells back up the stairs. He was about to go up the stairs, but he turned around and made his way into the kitchen. They seem to go through a lot of bulbs in this house. They were sometimes replacing two bulbs a week in various lamps, lamps that had gone what seemed like years without needing a new bulb in their apartment. He can only assume it has something to do with the age of the house, but he can not find anything to back that up on the internet, and he has looked hard for evidence.

Peter meets Maggie standing just inside the bedroom, waiting for him and the bulb. "I'll change it," Peter offers. He is taller than Maggie by quite a bit, making it easier for him to reach the light bulb. When he reaches into the wall sconce, he makes a startling discovery. The bulb is already unscrewed. It is just sitting in the socket, not actually engaged with any of the threads. There is little wonder as to why the light did not turn on. The question is why the light bulb was already unscrewed.

With a frown, Peter threads the light bulb into place, shielding his eyes as the old bulb comes to life. "What happened?" Maggie asks him, confused.

"The bulb must have come unscrewed. I put it back, and it works good as new," Peter answers her, looking away from the bright bulb.

"How does that happen?" Maggie asks, frowning. She has lived with electricity all of her life. She has never seen a bulb just unscrew itself. She has never heard of that happening either. If she were a betting woman, she would bet that not too many people have ever heard of a self-removing light bulb.

"I have no idea. And no, it is not the ghost," Peter answers, looking back at the light. "Maybe since it is a twist switch, the threads are getting turned every time we turn on the light, slowly pushing the light bulb out of place."

"Sure..." Maggie answers with skepticism. She looks up at Peter through her lashes, hip cocked and arms crossed. Her skepticism is portrayed in every line on her frame.

"It could happen. Otherwise, I have no idea. I'm going to chalk it up to the fact that our house is old as dirt and the wiring has not been updated since the seventies. Anything could have caused the bulb to move," Peter smiles down at Maggie. Kissing her gently on her lips, he walks off to the bathroom to get ready for bed.

***

It is not until the next day that Maggie thinks about the light again. It is as she stands in her craft room, sorting through papers. There is a quilt pattern that she was looking for, one that she had put in a safe spot so she would not lose it. *Yeah, like that ever works,* she thinks to herself. She has gone through and checked all of the lights in the house, making sure they are all tightly in their sockets. Most of them were loose, some by a lot. One fell out of the lamp as she was reaching for it. She was lucky to catch the bulb, without breaking it, before it hit the floor. Shattered lightbulbs can be dangerous to clean.

Gathering her papers into a pile on the cutting board that she uses to make her quilts, Maggie makes a pile and sets them down. They are quilt patterns that she intends to make. Leaving the room, she switches off the light on the wall and begins going downstairs. She goes to the landing before she remembers she wanted to bring one of the patterns downstairs so she did not forget to take it to her mother's on the weekend. *I'd forget my head if it were not attached to me.*

Walking back upstairs and into the craft room, Maggie does not even bother to turn on the light. It is not that dark in the room. There is some light coming through the window and its sheer curtain. After a few minutes of squinting in the dim light to find a pattern, she mutters to herself, "I should have just turned on the light."

As if in confirmation that there is definitely a ghost messing with her lights, the lights come on. The wall switch had been flipped from the off position to the on position. There is no one else in the house besides River and herself. It is the ghost and there was no way that Peter was going to believe her. At least it is a helpful ghost.

"Thank you," Maggie shyly says as she quickly finds the right pattern, turns off the light, and makes her way downstairs. If it is a ghost, there is no reason not to be polite. After all, he or she just helped out when they did not have to. Maybe being polite would keep the bulbs in the sockets. If there is not a ghost, well, no harm no foul, Maggie is fine talking to herself.

When Peter came home, he did not believe Maggie's story about the helpful ghost. "It was probably just an electrical glitch. Maybe the switch was not fully engaged and slipped back into the on position," he reasons. Maggie would believe it, but the timing is just too coincidental. Just as she needed help, the electricity fritzed just right to help her. A ghost is more believable than that and she told him that. Peter just pats her on the top of her head, gives her a kiss, and moves on. No sense in arguing about something that neither of them is willing to budge on.

***

Maggie is up in her craft room, cutting strips for a railroad quilt when Peter comes bolting up the stairs. He is pale and out of breath. He looks like he saw the ghost that he kept denying existed. "Okay, you're right. We're haunted," Peter gasps.

"What happened?" Maggie asks as she steps out of the craft room and leans against the door jam.

"I was watching television with the lights off, and all of a sudden all of the lights on that tree lamp of yours turned on. All five of them. No one was near the lamp," Peter explains. "I could even hear the nob turning. Someone or something turned the nob on the lamp, not once or twice, but three times, turning on all of the lights."

"Did you say thank you?" Maggie asks him.

"Uh, no. I did not say thank you to the ghost for scaring the ever-living hell out of me."

"I think the ghost is trying to be helpful. When they turned on the lights for me, it was because I was struggling to see my papers in the dark. I think the ghost was trying to prevent you from getting eye strain by watching television in the dark," Maggie reasons.

"You think the ghost is helping us," Peter deadpans. "You do remember that the ghost unscrewed all of the light bulbs, right? How is that helpful?"

"It made me have to check on all the lights? Okay, maybe helpful is a bit of a strong term for the ghost's actions. Maybe, not harmful, playful might even be a better term."

"Well, we'll see. If it gets violent, then we're gonna have to see about calling an exorcist or something. I'm not going to have a spirit or a ghost hurting us or River."

"I'm sure it will be fine. We've been here for over six months, and the ghost hasn't hurt us yet," Maggie reasons. She has faith that the ghost is not out to cause harm, but just to get some attention.

Burnt Dinner — 1975

Even though it hurt Kitty to just breathe, she still manages to go to work the next morning, and the morning after that. She keeps working, and keeps struggling to keep herself and her family afloat. It does not get any easier until Teddy finally sobers up enough to go to a temporary work agency and help to contribute to the family again.

Every morning, he would leave at the same time as Kitty. While Kitty rides the bus to her work and then was driven to the houses she is to work on from there, Teddy drives himself to the Temporary Employment Agency. From there, if they have employment for him for the day, he travels to the place they send him to work. If not, he would either go home or to the bar. While there might not be money for electricity, he always finds just enough money for a beer or two.

This makes it a little more difficult for Annie to go to the library. She never knew what time Teddy might be coming home, so she restricts her library visits to the weekends when her mother can go with her. To help out around the house, Annie takes to cleaning.

She spends every day tackling one room at a time, sweeping, dusting, and vacuuming. She takes care to get all the dishes done before her Mom comes home. She does the best she can to make life a little bit easier for Kitty. Annie does not think it was very fair that Mom has to work so hard and then come home and work some more. Dad does not have to do that, so why should Mom? She never voices her concerns though. She knows the consequences of that foolish action.

Sometimes she would become perplexed as to where things would go and have to decide on her own as to where they might belong. It was one such decision that caused so many problems one night. Annie is not sure where the envelopes belong. They could go in the drawer in the kitchen since bills are written there. Or they could go upstairs in the small office that her dad kept but did not really use. They could even go under the cabinet, with all the pens and pencils.

Annie decides that the envelopes went under the cabinet with the pens and pencils. You have to use a pen or a pencil to write on the envelope, so it makes sense to put them together. She promptly forgets to worry about her decision.

Annie is upstairs in her room, reading when she hears her father slamming drawers in the kitchen. He has been home half the day, having come back from the bar when he ran out of money and could no longer convince people to buy him a drink. He is angry and likely to take it out on anyone he sees until he finally just passes out. She decides she would stay put until she is called for dinner by her mother.

When Kitty comes home, she finds Teddy in a rage. He is seated on the couch, staring at the blank television screen, scowling. She assumes it is something to do with whatever job, or lack of job, that he had to do that day and decides to quietly go past him and start dinner. He does not make eye contact with her as she slinks by him and she is grateful for that.

Kitty has just put the vegetables in a hot pan with the chicken when Teddy comes into the kitchen. "Why did you do it?" he growls.

"Do what?" Kitty is completely confused as to what he means. Why did she add vegetables to the chicken? Why did she avoid talking to him? Why did she marry him? The first two she can answer, the third, she is not so sure anymore.

"Why'd you hide the envelopes?" Teddy stays just in the kitchen door, not close enough for him to touch her, but close enough that if he wanted to, she would not get away. Kitty can feel the trap closing in on her.

"I didn't think I did. I always leave them in the drawer," Kitty answers. She turns her back on the food she was making. She wants to keep an eye on him. There was not much she can do if he decides to attack her, but she wants something of a chance. She wants to see him coming.

"I found them under the cabinet, with the pens," Teddy's face is beginning to get red with his rage. It should not have been anything to get upset about, but for him, it is. He wanted to write a check to the electric company. Kitty had hidden the envelopes from him. Now she was lying about it. *That's just like her. She can't take any responsibility for herself. She'll say anything to avoid responsibility,* Teddy thinks to himself. He knows it is not true, but he still thinks it.

"Oh, Annie has been helping out around the house. I'm sure she just figured that's where they belong," Kitty laughs nervously. She immediately regrets mentioning Annie. What if he should decide to punish her. Kitty would never forgive herself if Annie got hurt.

"It's Annie's fault? Annie is a child. You are supposed to be cleaning the house, not her," Teddy growls even louder. His words are getting harder to understand, the louder he gets.

It is then that Kitty smelled the vegetables burning. Spinning around quickly, she finds dark smoke coming from the pan that she was supposed to be watching and stirring. "Shit, the food," she said as she lifts the pan off the brazier that she has been using since the electric was turned off, and begins trying to salvage the meal.

"You're useless. Can't cook, pushes the cleaning off on a kid," Teddy snaps. He grabs her arm, yanking her away from the stove. She does not have time to let go of the pan before she goes flying, dragging what would have been the night's dinner with her.

Teddy glares at her as though the resulting mess is her fault. "Never turn your back on me while I'm talking to you. You are pathetic. Everything you touch is an absolute disaster. You don't deserve to be a mother. You don't deserve to be a wife. You certainly don't deserve to be my wife. Get this shit cleaned up."

Teddy stalks out of the kitchen as though she threw the food on the floor, as though it were her temper that caused the mess. She can not help the tears that fall as she cleans the kitchen floor. By the time she starts a second dinner, she has herself under control. She had to keep it under control for Annie. Everything she does is for Annie.

When Kitty calls Annie down for dinner, it is not the chicken and vegetables that Annie had been expecting. Instead, it is macaroni and cheese with hot dogs. Teddy does not join them, but instead had left for a walk and had not returned yet. They are not holding dinner for him. Annie is not going to complain about it. She had heard her parents fight in the kitchen. She knew it was her fault. She would try to do better for her Mom.

The Crayon — 2007

"Maggie, has this always been like this?" Peter calls over to his wife. Maggie is cooking dinner, making her favorite Chicken and Cheese Pasta dish. It had chicken, pasta, cheese, and broccoli in it. The name kind of gives the dish away, but it is fast, easy, and reheats well. It is everything that someone was looking for in a workday dinner.

"Has what always been like this?" she calls back, without looking up. She knows he is just on the other side of the room, looking under the cabinets. They have some ant traps down there, somewhere. With the onset of autumn, the ants look like they are trying to take over the house.

"It looks like someone colored on the drawer," Peter answers as he stands up. His knees crack loud enough to be heard across the room and Maggie winces in sympathy. It sounds less than comfortable. At least he found the ant traps.

"Do you think one of the kids might have done it when they were over last weekend?" Maggie has a hard time believing that the kids would have colored on the drawers, but kids are kids, and they don't always act rationally.

"I don't think so. We were both with them the whole time. Besides, they know better than to color on anything except for paper. And this looks like scribbles, not hearts or flowers like the girls have been making," Peter says, thinking back over which kids they had over that weekend. It was the two oldest girls in the group. One was Maggie's sister's kid, and the other was her brother's kid. Between Peter, Maggie, and the two girls, they made the Oldest Club since they are all the oldest in the family.

"Maybe we just didn't notice it?" Maggie is still making dinner, so she does not go over and check it out. She trusts her husband's assessment of the mess. It is unlikely that they just missed a mess on their cabinets, but sometimes they were both blind about problems in the house. They expected to see clean cabinets, so they did if they were actually clean or not.

"Yeah, maybe," Peter says as he goes to grab the WD-40 from under a different cabinet. That got crayon off surfaces better than any of the traditional cleaners, and they knew this from experience. When the oldest was just a baby, she was over and decided to color on the walls. It was especially embarrassing for Maggie who was sitting directly in front of her when Cally simply turned from the coloring book and took to the walls. They learned a lot that day.

"Or it could be the ghost," Maggie continues to speculate. Peter does not bother to entertain that possibility. Instead, he sprayed the crayon marks, waited a couple of minutes, and wiped them away. WD-40 always worked like a charm to remove crayons. It was far more effective than anything else that they had tried.

***

The following day finds Peter completely perplexed, staring at the drawer that he just cleaned the night before. This time Maggie stands with him. "Could you have not gotten it all, last night?" she asks him, not taking her eyes off the cabinet. They are still in their pajamas, having just woken up. River is outside, enjoying the sunrise and the birds singing, completely oblivious to her parents' perplexion.

They are both staring at the drawer. It is covered in red, blue, and green crayon marks. It is almost as though someone had stood there and rubbed the crayons on the drawer until the crayon was gone. There is no pattern to it, just scribbles. It seems unlikely to be something that was missed. It looks different enough than the previous night's scribbles for Peter to know it is not just a failure for the crayon to wash off.

Peter just looks over at Maggie. It is clear that this was not something that Peter would have missed when he cleaned the crayon marks yesterday. "Maybe you got the first layer, and then another layer showed up after the WD-40 worked on the drawer some more. I know you wiped it off, but there might still have been a residue that brought the wax up to the surface," Maggie tries for a reasonable voice, but she has one real thought as to what happened.

"Next you're gonna say that the ghost did it. That he or she is trying to get our attention," Peter says. He knows what his wife is thinking, even if she is reluctant to say it. After having been together for what feels like forever sometimes, he knew exactly what she was going to say most of the time. Hell, he hears her voice in his head even when she's not there.

"Well, it would make sense—more sense than you missing a whole bunch of crayon marks after you cleaned the drawer yesterday. Or, maybe you thought you cleaned this one, but you actually cleaned the one next to it? Maybe they both had marks on them, and you didn't notice this one last night," Maggie is trying her best to sound reasonable, staying skeptical. It is not easy for her.

"Maybe. Doubtful, but maybe. That still leaves us to wonder which of the kids did it. And we're not asking their parents. I don't want them to get in trouble for being kids. I'll just clean this up then put a pot of coffee on if you want to hop in the shower," Peter concedes.

With a quick kiss, Maggie walks to the upstairs bathroom to take her shower and Peter starts cleaning the drawers again. He makes sure to check every single one for crayon marks this time. Before Maggie starts her shower, he fills the coffee craft and makes coffee for the morning. He might not drink it, but he knows how much Maggie loves fresh coffee, and he loves her.

As the coffee brews, Peter walks around the downstairs, checking all of the walls for any other signs that the kids might have doodled on anything that they were not supposed to. The nearest thing he finds to that is the book of post-it cards that all have hearts and flowers on them. It was tucked in a glass vase. He left it there. He would show Maggie, and they would leave it be. They always keep everything that the kids give them or make for them, no matter how little. One day they'll know how much those little things matter to Maggie and Peter.

Smiling, Peter pulls it out of the vase and flips through the post-its. He finds that if he flips them quickly, he can watch the hearts and flowers fall from the top of the paper to the bottom. He is pretty sure which kid did this. The oldest, Maggie's sister's kid, Cally, is an inspiring artist. She is also a couple of years older than Maggie's brother's kid, Nikki.

Peter hears the shower turn off and smiles. Maggie would be down in a couple of minutes. Filling a mug with coffee and creamer, Peter sets up a spot for Maggie to enjoy her coffee and bagel before work. Feeding River, he ensures that they can all enjoy breakfast at the same time. It is one of his favorite things, seeing his wife and his dog happy. There is just one more touch to do to make everything perfect. Peter sets the Post-it pad next to Maggie's mug. He would have to remember to put it back in the vase.

Maggie is cheery when she makes her way back to the kitchen. Her hair is still wet and her cheeks are flushed from the hot shower she took. She is beautiful. She smiles at the cup of coffee and then cooed at the post-it notes. "Cally?" She guesses.

"I can't say for sure. I found them tucked in a vase. They're not signed, but I suspect they are Cally's work," Peter answers as he hands Maggie a plate with a sliced bagel, warmed but not toasted.

"So weird. But, I love it. We'll have to hang onto it for her."

"Like we ever get rid of anything the kids ever make. We have a refrigerator covered in their art," Peter laughs.

"That's true," Maggie says just before biting into her perfect bagel. She is a lucky woman, this is heaven. She glances over at the refrigerator and the art that is displayed there. There are construction paper hearts, letters, and hand turkeys. When they ran out of room, they put the oldest art pieces of each kid in a folder, saving them for all of time. They make sure that there is at least one piece of art per kid on the refrigerator at all times. No one is ever left out at their house. There are no favorites.

Play Quietly — 1975

Annie is primarily a solitary child. That is how it is when you are the new person to the block and school had not quite started yet. You do not have a lot of opportunities to make friends unless your parents know their parents. However, sometimes the universe throws out a bone and helps a kid along. For Annie, that help came in the form of Bobby.

Bobby is the boy from across the street. He is a year older than her, but they would be going to the same grade in school. They are almost polar opposites of each other, and that might be why they became such solid friends. Where Annie is quiet and reserved, Bobby is loud and outgoing. Annie likes to read, but Bobby likes to play sports and games. It is a friendship that was meant to be.

One of their favorite games to play is Pirate Ships. This is a game of pretend where they would draw a map, leave clues and notes, and then try to find buried treasure. They take their time, drawing up various maps. Some show the route from each other's houses to the fabled treasure. Some show where the treasure was in the houses. Some take them all the way to the park, which Annie could go to, provided Bobby is with her.

It was one such day that they were following the maps from Bobby's house to Annie's house. Traipsing through the yard and down the driveway, they cry "Argh" between every sentence, laughing and having fun. They forgot to be quiet. Why should they worry about being quiet, Kitty and Teddy both left for work early in the morning.

It was unfortunate that Kitty had fallen ill while she was at work. Her co-workers insisted that she go to the hospital, but knowing her bruised back and neck, Kitty refused. Instead, she decided to simply head home and rest. She was sure that she would feel better by the next day.

Kitty did not check to see if Annie was up in her room. She figured that if she was, that was fine. If she was not, then she would be with Bobby, which was also fine. No one could expect a nine-year-old to just stay at home on a beautiful day. Taking some Tylenol, Kitty laid down on the couch with a cloth over her eyes, trying to will her body into feeling better before Teddy got home.

That's when she hears them. They are running up and down the driveway, screaming at the top of their lungs. "We're really going to find that treasure this time. ARGH!" Bobby cries out, enjoying his game.

"Definitely! ARGH!" Annie's laughter echoes down the driveway, ringing in Kitty's ears. She tries to ignore the two kids. After all, they are doing what kids do, they are playing. But after listening to them run the driveway for what felt like the fiftieth time, it is too much for Kitty.

Kitty throws off her cloth, now hot from the fever she is trying to deny having. She storms to the back door, throwing it open and banging it on the counter behind it. Kitty stomps across the deck and waits for a second for the two kids to come racing past her, one more time. "WILL YOU TWO PLEASE PLAY QUIETLY!" Kitty demands of them.

Kitty being home and yelling at them so surprises both of the children that they skid to a stop. "Ah, yeah. We'll be quiet. Sorry, Mom," Annie stammers. "I didn't know you were home."

Kitty takes a deep breath. It is not their fault they are behaving like children because they are children. "Yes, I just got home. I have a headache. I need you two to play quietly or play over at Bobby's house."

"We'll be quiet, Mrs. Koonz," Bobby answers. He does not want to go back home. His Dad was home and they would both find themselves doing chores, like raking grass cuttings or pulling weeds out of the flower bed.

Kitty gives them a tight smile, assessing the potential of them actually being quiet. With a deep breath, she goes back into the house to get a fresh cloth and go all the way up to her room. That way if they are loud, there is a lower chance she would hear them. As soon as Kitty was out of sight, Annie said, "We're gonna have to be quiet. The Indians might hear us and find our treasure first. We should write notes so they don't overhear us."

"You forgot to say 'argh" after your sentence," Bobby whispers back with a smile.

Smiling, Annie answers him, "Argh."

The two of them creep into Annie's house and take a notebook and some pencils from the phone stand. They spend the rest of the day, making almost no noise, just writing notes back and forth. They even take to sneaking up and down the driveway, practicing hiding from the Indians and traps that they make up in their imaginations.

They eat the snacks that Bobby had packed from his house for lunch, sitting under the shade of Annie's giant tree out back. They even eventually find a small treasure. It is a small silver ring. It may or may not have been a keychain at some point in its life, but for now, it was a priceless piece of jewelry.

Smiling and silently laughing, they eventually gather up their notes and the wrappers from their snacks and go their separate ways. All good games had to eventually come to an end. Dinner time is coming up fast, and neither of them want to miss it after being out and playing all day.

Annie watches Bobby leave to go to his house. She holds her smile until he is out of sight, but then drops it as though it were never there. Yes, she has a lot of fun with Bobby, but now it is time to come back to reality. Mom is not feeling well. She might not make dinner. Annie would help out and make dinner before Dad got home. There are a few things she could make. She would just have to make sure Mom got up before he got home, so it looks like Mom made the dinner.

The Note — 2008

It is New Year's Eve! With their large house, Maggie and Peter are the perfect people to throw a huge party. The cars line the driveway, and champagne flows like water. The ball drops, and so too do the hundreds of balloons that Maggie and Peter blew up and hung from the ceiling with netting.

Friends and family stay late into the night, and most of them stay until late morning. It is a great party and doubles not only as a New Year's Eve party but also as a housewarming party, even though the couple have been living in their home for a while now.

The best part is, there was no ghost activity. None of the lights flickered. There were no random Lego in the middle of the sitting room. The rocking chairs kept rocking, but they all had people in them when they rocked. The cabinets were never closed, but that was from people constantly opening them for a new cup or plate.

The next day dawns bright. There is not a single being in that house that rose with the sun, and none shined, not even River who had stayed up late with her humans. Unfortunately, everyone did have to get up and start their day. Time and glory waits for none, especially the hungover.

Once the last person is out of the house, Maggie and Peter assess their provisions. There is not a lot of food or drink left in the house. The niblings drank all of the milk. They may have also been responsible for the juice, but that could just as easily have been the adults. The bread was gone, as were the cold cuts and cheese. Pretty much anything that could be prepared quickly and just as quickly eaten was. They have to go grocery shopping.

Grocery shopping is one of the chores that Maggie and Peter share. They both enjoy shopping for food, hunting out the best deals, and finding those unique items that neither of them have tried before. This time, because they are buying so much food to restock, they stick to what they know and try to finish the task quickly.

Putting away the food is a challenge in its own right. River has to be distracted by a frozen treat, otherwise, she feels that she can help herself to whatever treats she finds. With a belly full of snacks from the previous night, she is nonetheless grateful for her frozen treats as they put their groceries away.

Everything is going great. The bread is in the built-in bread box. The pantries are full once again, and Maggie is making room in the refrigerator for all of the food they had bought. They sometimes went overboard, like this time. Turning around to ask Peter about a bottle of syrup she found tucked in the back of the refrigerator, she comes to a stop when she sees Peter taking apart the breadbox drawer.

"What are you doing?" Maggie asks Peter. She is not accusing, she is confused and needs clarification as to what was going on.

"You forgot to close the drawer and I ran into it. I tried to close it, and it wouldn't close. I want to find out why," Peter answers distractedly. He is peering up from under the drawer, looking at the track.

"I closed the drawer," Maggie answers a little defensively. She knows she closed the drawer because it was a two-step process. First, she has to close the metal slide that was on the top of the breadbox. Then she can close the drawer itself. You could not close the drawer without closing the top first.

"Found what was keeping it open," Peter says as he pulls out a piece of cardboard. Before he looks at it, he closes the drawer, testing it to make sure it runs smoothly on its tracks. Maggie finishes what she was doing at the refrigerator, and then crosses over to look at the cardboard with Peter. What they see drew a chill from them both.

The cardboard is an old game board. It is Chutes and Ladders to be specific. That is not the bone-chilling part, that is what they find on the back. There, written in crayon and the messy handwriting of a young child is a note.

Help me. Help me. Save me.
   Please save me.

"Well, that's terrifying," Maggie says, reading the note.

"I'm sure it was just a prank that one of the kids from the previous owners was playing. A game. It does not mean anything," Peter says, shaking slightly as he holds the game board. He has a hard time taking his eyes off the bright red crayon note.

"Right," Maggie sounds skeptical. "How did we never find the note before now? We use that drawer all the time."

"It must have been knocked loose when I hit the drawer. I did hit it rather hard. I'm going to have a bruise," Peter smiles down at Maggie. He is trying to distract her from how anxious the note left him, and how scared it left her.

"Right. It got knocked loose. And I know I closed that drawer. I don't leave drawers open, like some people I know," Maggie smiles back at him. It is easier to be distracted by Peter than it is to deal with the note.

"Well, either way, the drawer is fixed now. Nothing else is behind it, or on the tracks. I checked. We will just get rid of this, and move on. River wants a walk." Peter goes to toss the game board in the kitchen trash but see Maggie tense up. "I'll throw it away outside. No sense in having it take up space in the kitchen trash."

"That sounds like a good idea. That's a big board and the trash day is almost a full week away," Maggie agrees. While Peter throws that away, Maggie gathers River's leash and harness. They all had a lot of calories to walk off from the previous night.

Mom Gets Hurt — 1975

A week later and Kitty is still plagued with headaches and nausea. She feels weak and achy throughout her body. Her co-workers suspect that she might be pregnant, but she knows it is not that. She remembered how she felt when she was pregnant with Annie. She could almost feel the baby grow and develop from day one. She was nauseous and tired, but not achy and irritable, like she is now. Sure, every pregnancy is different, but considering she just had her monthly, she is pretty sure that is not it. The problem is that she was not sure what is wrong.

What she knows was that she can not go to the hospital or to her doctor's office for it. She simply did not have the money for that type of expense. Teddy had been carrying the health insurance before he was fired. While Kitty works full-time, her job did not offer insurance. Teddy has not been at his new job long enough to qualify for insurance. This meant that whatever it is, she is left to deal with it on her own.

Kitty's health continues to deteriorate as the week continues. Soon, it was all she can do to keep down some water and have a few crackers before nausea overtook her. With nausea comes dizziness. It was one such spell that caused a nearly fatal accident for Kitty. She was cleaning the stairs at one of the houses she cleaned when the nausea struck her. In her rush to reach the bathroom before throwing up, she tripped on the stairs, striking her head against the wall. She hit her head hard and collapsed on the stairs.

It is her co-worker, Mary Ann, who had heard her strike the wall and decides to check on her. When she finds Kitty, she runs and gets a cool towel to place over her face to help revive her. She also calls their manager and tells him about Kitty's fall, as she is supposed to do. When their manager, Mr. Axler, arrives he finds Kitty sitting in a kitchen chair, ashen and haggard.

Standing over her, he begins to ask her about what is going on. Kitty had been his top employee, and now she is becoming a problem. "What's going on, Kitty? Are you sick? Pregnant? Tired?"

"I... I don't know," Kitty stammers. She knows at that moment she feels tired; tired and scared. She is pretty sure that Mr. Axler is going to fire her. It is not her fault that she is sick, but without a doctor's notice, how is she to explain or prove anything?

"I think you have been working too hard. I think that you need to take some time off. We'll hold your position here for a while, but you need to rest up. You have been pulling over sixty hours a week, most weeks. Last week you completely missed the bathrooms at one of the houses and I had to send another woman to finish your house. This week, we find you like this. Go home," Mr. Axler says. He did not fire her, but he might as well have. She would not be able to return to her position, and they both know it. She is a liability, not finishing her houses and now getting hurt at a client's house. Her days working as a housekeeper with Mr. Axler are over.

Teddy is not home when Kitty finally walked into her home. He still has a couple of hours left at work. Annie is not home either. She is most likely with Bobby, either at his house or at the park. Kitty decides to go upstairs and take a nap. Maybe she would feel better after a nap because, at that moment, she feels that her world is crashing down.

It was unfortunate that Kitty forgot to set an alarm to wake her up before Teddy had gotten home and that Annie did not realize that she was home so to wake her up to make dinner. Instead, it is Teddy who wakes her by yanking her out of bed. He is drunk, as usual, and furious that he came home to find that dinner was not ready for him.

Teddy does not ask what was wrong with Kitty. He does not care when the beer has him. Instead, all he sees was that his wife is in her nightgown, in bed, during the day while he is hungry after working all day. Kitty falls to the floor, stunned and dazed. She would have hit her dresser if it were not for the fact that Teddy still has her by her arm. He yanks on her once again, this time forcing her to stand.

Dragging her out of the bedroom, he begins to force her down the stairs. Her struggles begin to irritate him as they reach the landing and she almost manages to push him out the full-sized window that was nearly level with the floor there. Swinging her in front of him, he pushes her.

Kitty was never a big girl. She has even be called petite or elven in stature. When Teddy pushes her from the landing, her small size works against her. The force of his shove is enough to send her flying, striking her head on the overhang above the stairs. For a second time that day, the darkness claims her.

This time when she wakes up, she is alone. There is blood on the stairs and some on the walls. There is blood on the floor. There was a lot of blood. It is hard to believe that it all came from her and that she is not dead. At least she does not think she is dead, her head hurt too much for her to be dead. Her mind is fuzzy, and her stomach is once again upset. Throwing up, then and there is the only option available to her, so she did. Then, once done, she staggers up and gathers her cleaning supplies. She has to get it clean before the stain sets and Annie found her like this.

Cracks in the Walls — 2008

Peter is carrying a basket of laundry from the bedroom to the basement. Laundry is one of Peter's chores at home. He carries the basket with both hands, arms in front of him. This load is Maggie's dirty laundry, and he would have to be careful to make sure he checks her pockets before throwing everything in the washing machine. Maggie has a tendency to leave stuff in her pockets.

Laundry had been Maggie's chore for the first ten years of their relationship and she expected to continue to do the laundry in their home. While it was not one of her favorite chores, it was nice being able to immediately curl up with a blanket hot from the dryer after the laundry was done. That was until they realized that the washer and drier would be installed on a pedestal and her height became an issue.

Calling the pad that the washer and drier sat on in the basement a pedestal is a little excessive. It is a pad of cement about a foot and a half off the basement floor. It was most likely built like that to prevent ruining the washer and drier if the basement flooded. It is the only place where the washer and drier could be installed as it was also where the hookups are installed. Moving the hookups was not a cost-friendly option. The downside to this is that now Maggie can not reach into the washer to get the clothes out.

Oh, Maggie tries. She would boost herself up and hang over the edge of the washer, diving headfirst into the machine to get the clothes. Peter almost fell over laughing, watching her little feet kick as she struggled to get all the clothes out and into the dryer the first time they did laundry in the house. Sure, she has a small stool to help her reach, but it is not high enough. She can have bring the one from the kitchen down to the basement for laundry, but that is more work than it is worth to her. Plus, it works out to her favor with Peter now doing the laundry.

As he walks down the stairs, he notices a crack in the overhang on the stairs. It stretches from the middle of the overhang over to the left-hand wall. A little bit of the white plaster that is under the salmon-colored paint is visible. He could only hope it was not a new crack. "Maggie? How long has this crack been here?" Peter calls out.

From the kitchen, he could hear an exasperated sigh, "What crack?"

"This crack," he calls back. He smiles to himself, now she would have to come find him to see what he is looking at. He knows it irritates her just a little bit, just enough to be charming when he smiles at her, which he would and she would smile and sigh, and life would be good.

Maggie comes through the living room quickly, nimbly stepping over River as she lay in the middle of the floor. When she goes up the stairs, Peter moves over a little bit so that she can stand on the stair with him and they could look at the crack together.

Maggie looks at the crack, and then around the crack, looking for clues as to how long the damage has been there and how deep it goes. "I don't see any plaster dust. I think the mark is cracked paint, only. I haven't noticed it before, but it could have been there since before we bought the house. I don't really know. I'll worry about it if we see plaster dust or if it gets worse. The house is old, it probably just did some settling and cracked the paint. No worries, right?"

"Is it just me, or is there red underneath the pink paint?" Peter squints his eyes to get a better look.

"I don't see any red. If there is, maybe it is just fresher paint than what we can currently see, if that makes any sense. Paint that has not faded from exposure."

Peter had to admit that her answer makes sense. There are a few other cracks in the walls that they have also noticed. They seem to just appear, but they could not find any serious damage, just cracked paint. There is some cracked paint by the bedroom door, some by the front door, and now this.

They would just have to watch it and make sure it did not get worse. If it got worse, then they might be stuck repairing the plaster, and that would be a chore.

The overhang crack stuck with Peter though. Not only is there the crack but there is an indent in the overhang. Whoever lived in the house before them had to have been tall to have made that indent, either that or thrown something, damaging that section. Peter was tall, and he had difficulty reaching the spot.

The stairs themselves have a little bit of a creepy, scary feel to them. The window that was right off the landing all but invites people to fall out of it. It was less than a foot from the bottom of the landing and a full five feet tall. Some of the stairs have rolled edges to them where there are cracks caused by wear over time, adding to the danger. There are even cracks in the plaster on the wall directly after the stairs, where the coat closet stands, almost as though a body had landed there once, hard. It is not hard for Peter to imagine someone falling down the stairs.

At least they would have a railing to try to catch hold of on their way down. Peter thinks to himself as he continues down the stairs. He could even see where one of the banister rails has been replaced at some time. It is a slightly different color than the other rails and it is at a slight angle from the rest of them. He can picture a child playing with that post, accidentally putting too much pressure on it and breaking it. He can also picture someone grabbing it on their way down the steps, snapping it under their weight. He prefers the image of the child in his mind.

Home Schooled — 1975

Now that Kitty has no job thanks to her frequent headaches and dizzy spells, she is relegated to staying home during the day. She would wake Annie up for school, cook breakfast for the family, and then get chores done. She is frequently done cleaning before noon, giving her the time she needs to rest and recover.

At first, this is a relief, almost a vacation. She could feel her strength returning and the frequency of her attacks lessening. Soon though, staying home became a trial in itself. Teddy insists that if she was not working outside of the house, she would have to work inside the house, and her task would be to teach Annie.

Annie has not shown any trouble in her new school. She is enjoying her classes and has a friend in Bobby. The friendship that they had developed during the summer continued once they started school. Kitty feels that being in a formal school setting with people her age would be best for Annie. It would help her develop confidence and peer coping skills. Kitty is therefore shocked when when Teddy calls the school and pulls Annie from her classes for Maggie to home school.

Kitty feels very under prepared to teach Annie from home. She manages to find the appropriate textbooks, workbooks, and lesson plans. They are expensive but necessary for home-schooling a child according to the state, or at least Kitty's understanding of the laws. The books are also something that Kitty needed, having completed her high school education over a decade before, and not recalling much of her education.

Kitty has no formal training as a teacher. She did not even do the training for the new hires when she worked as a housekeeper. She has not taught anyone anything in a formal environment for so long, she barely remembers how to do it. She is going to have to rely on Annie to tell her what she needs from Kitty.

Annie is dismayed to find that she has to leave her friends and the routine that going to school had given her. She knows better than to yell and argue about the decision, but that does not stop her from being heartbroken and upset in the safety of her room. Once she calms down, she figures there had to be some sort of an upside to homeschooling, she would see Mom more often. That is the only upside she could think of. That and the hope that she might be able to spend more time at the library now.

***

The first few days of homeschooling are challenging. Kitty and Annie have to come up with a plan, a routine to help them accomplish the learning that they need to do. They decide to do the classes at the kitchen table. They would wait until Teddy leaves for work, then they would pull out the books that they would need and start learning together. They would work from nine in the morning, until noon. Then they would stop for lunch and picking back up from one until four in the afternoon.

The hardest part of this new routine is the classes themselves. Annie is more than happy to spend her time learning about the sciences and literature. She would often advocate for spending more time on those subjects, meanwhile, her maths skills are slipping behind those of her peers. Kitty has a hard time convincing Annie, and truth be told, herself, to focus on those subjects that hold little to no interest for either of them.

If the work becomes too stressful for the day, the pair would simply stop and do something else. Often this reset time is spent going for walks or working on a craft. Kitty is able to use these activities as credits for physical education and art classes, giving them a dual purpose.

As the weather gets colder, walks became less frequent. Instead, they would go into the attic where there was more room, and play with a ball, bouncing it back and forth between each other. It is one of Annie's favorite ways to spend her lunch hour, playing with her Mom.

The worst part is that now Kitty was once again left to bare up under additional stresses. While she loves having Annie home with her all day, she is still expected to keep the house clean and have dinner ready by the time Teddy gets home. This often leaves her choosing between helping Annie with her classwork or handling the housework that she is expected to do. All too often she finds herself leaving Annie to work alone.

The headaches and dizzy spells begin to increase as these stresses continue for months. It is only a matter of time before the headaches became migraines and Kitty is unable to do any of her duties, either as a teacher or as a housewife. It was on those days that Annie does her best to help out. She would clean for the first few hours of the day, leaving her mother to rest in her darkened bedroom. Then she would sit and read in her room.

It was a rough day for Kitty when Teddy came home earlier than normal from work. Annie had spent the morning cleaning the kitchen. She had done her classwork and was up in the attic, bouncing a ball against the wall to herself. Kitty is laying in the dark with a damp towel over her eyes. She hears the car pull into the driveway. When she glances at the clock in terror, she sees that Teddy was home a full two hours early. Something must have happened at the shop.

She quickly runs to the attic, throwing her towel into the bathroom as she passes it. She makes it up the stairs to Annie just in time to hear Teddy come through the front door. She would be okay, they would just explain that this is part of the curriculum, physical education.

"Hello!" Teddy bellows, finding no one downstairs.

"We're up here, in the attic," Kitty calls back. "We're just finishing up Phys. Ed." Kitty can hear Teddy's heavy steps as he ascends the staircase. She fears what she would see as he watches them toss the ball back and forth. The sense of relief she feels as she watches him smile is almost enough to bring her to her knees.

"Can I play, too?" Teddy asks. The look on Annie's face says it all. She is delighted to play with her Dad. It has been so long since they were all able to just play together.

Laughter in the Attic — 2008

prong, sprong, sprong...

There is a ball bouncing against the floor and wall in the attic. At least that is what it sounds like to Maggie and Peter as they lay in bed. It had woken them up with a start, even River is awake, staring up at the ceiling. None of them are moving to investigate the noise.

Peter glances over to the alarm clock. It is four in the morning. The alarm clock would be going off in a couple of hours, but this time he is already awake. There was no way he is going to sleep listening to the ball bounce around up there. He just hopes that it does not break anything. His record collection is up there.

The worst part about the whole thing is, they do not own a rubber bouncy ball. Especially not one that makes that particular *Sprong* noise. It brought to his mind the image of the red dodge ball type balls. The ones that would hit you hard, but conformed around a person so that it did not break bones, just left a large red mark that you had to walk around school with for the next hour. It is a very particular type of sound.

A few minutes after the noise suddenly started, it suddenly stops. The ball may have bounced for all of five minutes, but it was five terrifying minutes that guaranteed no more sleep for Peter or Maggie. River decides that since it was done, she is going back to sleep. A dog needed her rest.

Maggie and Peter go downstairs to watch television and relax after their early morning scare. Once it is light out, they decide that they can investigate the attic. Maybe there is a ball up there that they did not remember buying. Maybe it has a battery and that is what made it jump and bounce last night.

Maybe a raccoon or squirrel broke in decided to play with the ball. Neither of them believed it, but the alternative is literally haunting.

Together they go to the attic door. River, seeing her parents stand before the door gets up and joins them. With a deep breath, they open the door, flicked on the light, and ascend the stairs.

The front part of the attic had been converted to Peter's man cave. On the slanted walls there are band posters, the vinyl kind that hung on railings and in bar windows. There are framed and signed posters on the low vertical walls. His computer is up there, along with his record collection. What is not up there is a ball. They even check the other side of the attic, the storage area, but there was no ball.

As they turn to leave the attic, a young girl's laughter fills the room. It is the happy, joyful laughter of a child having fun. It would have been one of the greatest sounds in the world if only there were a child attached to it. Instead, it is one of the creepiest. It lasts only a few seconds, but it is long enough to give the pair goosebumps and make Peter's hair stand on end. Even River looks unsettled.

Rushing downstairs, the small family take refuge in the kitchen, as though the ghost could not possibly go there. "Okay, maybe there is an explanation," Peter says, not believing it himself.

"I am all ears," Maggie deadpanned. She is eager to hear anything that makes what she just experienced make sense.

"Maybe we are in one of those acoustical locations where we have an easy time hearing things that are actually happening at a distance. I heard about some areas that make it possible to have a quiet conversation all the way across a busy room. And both of us remember that one driveway where if we stood at the corner of the house, we could hear what people were saying across the street and at the corner. Maybe we're hearing what is going on at another house," Peter reasons.

"Maybe..." Maggie thought for a moment. "But, if that were the case, wouldn't we have heard something before? And who plays with a ball at four in the morning?"

"Children?" Peter guesses. They did not have children, so any answer with children soundes like a plausible answer, not that he could picture his niblings playing with a bouncy ball at four in the morning.

"I am certain that if I ask my siblings if their kids play with their bouncy balls at four in the morning, in the attic, the answer will be no," Maggie leans back against the countertop, crossing her arms over her chest. She's not backing down from her belief that whatever is happening, it is definitely supernatural.

"Maybe?" Peter shrugs. He knows he is not going to win this.

"Maybe I'll go to the library and see if I can find out who lived in the house before us. Maybe if we know who this ghost is, we can help them move on and we can have the house to ourselves," Maggie suggests.

"Good luck," Peter wishes her as he began to get ready for work. Ghosts in the attic do not mean that either of them gets the day off work.

***

The following Saturday finds Maggie in the Heritage Room of the main branch of the library. She is working with one of the many volunteers who helps patrons find the information that they are looking for, quickly. Considering she has no idea where to look and nothing but the address of the house to go to, Maggie is certain she was going to need all the help that she could get.

It takes hours, but Valerie, the woman helping Maggie, is finally able to point her to some reference material about the home's previous owners. The details are scant, but it does paint an interesting picture of the house that they now call home. Making photocopies of the details, Maggie takes the work home to show Peter.

***

Sitting at the kitchen table, Peter looks over the notes that Maggie had made. There is not a lot to go on. It gives details of the house being built in 1912 and completed in 1913. The house was a wedding present from John Miller to his new wife, Hilda. There was a picture of them standing on the porch in celebration of their new home. It had been in the newspaper at the time.

As there were no announcements about them ever having children, they assumed that the ghost was not from them. Maggie had even found the death notice of Hilda and John Miller, and no children were mentioned there, either.

"John died in 1965. The house was empty for five years before it was bought by Robin McGuire. He turned it into a rental in 1972 after making heavy repairs and updates. Robin McGuire was Paul McGuire's dad, and Paul was who we bought the house from. There are no public records as to who rented the house from Robin or Paul. That would be in their personal records, and they are not obligated to show up those records. I asked about that," Maggie summarizes the work she had done.

"So, there is no way that we're gonna know who this ghost is unless we find actual evidence or they tell us," Peter summarizes her summary.

"We could call a ghost hunter," Maggie shrugs as though she had not looked into that already.

"No, no ghost hunters. Not even if they go by the name, Ghost Busters. We'll just deal with it for now." Paul draws the line at ghost hunters. He had seen them on television, and he did not want that in his house. "The ghost has not hurt anyone or broken anything. It will be okay."

Peter smiles at Maggie, and his confidence gave her confidence.

Hide and Seek — 1976

It is winter break for the kids that went to public school. For the kids like Annie, who are home-schooled, it is just winter. Annie tries to visit with her friend Bobby, but they grew apart throughout the school year and he is not in town over the break. It was a friendship that she greatly missed.

Annie and Bobby did try to make their friendship work. It was almost effortless during the summer. They saw each other every day. They played the same games. They expected the same things during the school year. Homeschooling messed that up for Annie.

Bobby is able to be involved in sports, and he takes to playing football and basketball. That does not leave a lot of time for Annie. His homework is daunting for a ten-year-old. That eats up what little time was left in his day so that even on the weekends, he is busy. Breaks like the winter break are filled with going to visit family. Annie was left behind.

Kitty became Annie's playmate, as well as her teacher and her mother. The two spend almost all of their time together when Kitty's headaches are not so debilitating. They play a lot of games together once their studies are done for the day. Besides board games and ball, one of their favorite games is hide and seek.

***

"Okay, my turn to count to one hundred. Then I'll find you!" Kitty calls out as Annie goes running off to hide. Annie had just found her sitting in the bathtub. It took Annie a couple of minutes to find Kitty in there. Typically Kitty hides behind doors or under the bed. Annie is better at hiding, but she gives herself a way most of the by laughing.

Kitty starts to count out loud and slowly. She lowers her voice as she goes, giving Annie more time to hide. She hears her daughter take off through the kitchen. When Kitty judges that enough time had passed, she calls out, "Ready or not, here I come!"

Kitty walks heavily as she wanders around the rooms that she knows Annie is not in. She takes the time to pick up some toys and toss them in the baskets where they belong, putting jackets in the closets. She can hear Annie giggling in the kitchen as she slowly works her way around the house. She makes sure to make it sound like she is going to look upstairs, treading hard on the first few steps.

Once she is certain that Annie thought she went upstairs, she silently pads her way down the stairs and through the living room. She shifts to her toes, eliminating any noise she makes as she steps through to the kitchen, peering under the table to where her daughter is hiding. With a shriek, Annie is off, laughing and trying to dodge her Mom, playing chase now.

Kitty manages to scoop Annie up as she dives to get past her. Pulling her daughter close to her, she begins to tickle her as she carries her to the living room sofa, intending to dump her on there and tickle her some more. They were only this size for so long, and then they grew too big to pick up and carry. Kitty is going to take advantage of it now.

As Kitty is carrying Annie to the couch that she sees him. It is Teddy, and he looks furious. He is home early, drunk, and he looks like he is spoiling for a fight. Kitty sobers immediately. She sets Annie down on her feet and spins her around so that Annie is facing Kitty. "Hide. Do not come out until I call you," Kitty instructs her, looking her in the eye to convey the sense of urgency she feels.

"Okay," Annie answers seriously. She had seen her Dad, too. She knows his temper. She wass going to run upstairs, but he would see her as she made the stairs. Instead, she bolts for the basement, leaving her mother to face the man by herself.

Annie runs through the kitchen, opening the basement door and quietly closing it behind her. She ghosts down the first set of stairs and stops. There is a small dried goods pantry on the landing just before the basement. It is knee height on an adult and has a small door. It is enclosed and easy to overlook from the basement. It is a great hiding spot, even if she never used it while playing with her Mom.

Closing the door behind her, she sits in the middle of the pantry in Indian Style. It is dark, but Annie is a big girl. She is not afraid of the dark. There are cobwebs and spiders, but Mom assured her that spiders wouldn't hurt her. When it gets loud upstairs, she closes her eyes and covers her ears. She tries to ignore the thump of her mother's body hitting the floor. She squeezes her ears harder to block out the cries.

Annie sat there for a long time. She heard her Dad call her name. It was a very slurred call. There were many words that she was not supposed to know attached to it. Her father is not satisfied with punishing her Mom for whatever happened. He wants to punish her, too. She wants to avoid that at all costs. She sits still, in the dark.

She wakes up hours later, not realizing that she had fallen asleep. She is laying on her side, head on her arms, legs tucked against her chest. She is covered in dirt, spiderwebs, and dust. Then she hears it, a knocking at the door. Someone is knocking on the pantry door. They know she is here. Then the door is opening. With a shot of terror, Annie sees a form in the doorway, and she has no way to escape. With relief washing through her body, she realizes it is her Mom. Mom found her. It must be safe now.

Mom is a little worse for wear. She is sporting a black eye and can barely open that eye. But she already has the bag of peas out of the freezer, so she is going to be okay. Her hair is disheveled, and her shirt is ripped. It could have been worse though. The two silently step into the backyard to catch the last of the sun and try to recover, together.

A Bump in the Basement — 2008

Peter and Maggie stand around it as though it might do something. After all, it did do something not too long ago. It appeared. They are both absolutely certain that what is in front of them now was not there before. Granted, they do not spend a lot of time in the basement. Hardly any, time, in reality. Just enough to do laundry and that is it. Sometimes they drop things off for storage there, provided it is something they are going to be getting rid of.

The problem with the basement is that it was dark and damp. It is not quite wet, although there are a few puddles that form when it rains hard. It was also low. The ceiling of the basement is around six feet high, making it dangerously low for Peter, who has just inches between him and the ceiling. The lights hang low, putting them at eye level for Peter. There are only two lights for the entire basement, casting parts of it in heavy shadow.

What they are looking at right now is directly between the light and a window, making it well-lit. They are standing to the right of the stairs, staring at a bump in the floor. It is a pretty good-sized bump, one that does not look like it could have been ignored before. Especially as it is directly in the path to the washer and dryer.

The bump itself is about a foot off the ground from the rest of the floor. There are cracks in the cement where it looks like pressure from underneath it pushed up. The paint on the floor is also cracked. They cannot not see what is under the bump, just that the bump now exists.

"I'm going back to the library. I am going to look up missing people and see if any of those missing people might have lived in this house," Maggie says, not taking her eyes off the bump.

"Yeah, that's going to be a long hunt. Meanwhile, I think I'm going to ignore this bump for a little bit and see if it goes away. If it does, then we can assume it was pressure from the water table under the house. If not, then I'm going to have to dig and find out what is under this. It might be a bust pipe or something," Peter lays out his plan to Maggie. He glances up at her. She is just slowly nodding, accepting the plan.

River did not join them in the basement.

***

Maggie is a welcome sight back at the library. She has always loved libraries, but she has never been in one as often as she has been in this one. This is the local main branch. It is a new building with large tinted windows that overlook the shelves. There are comfortable chairs and tables to read at. There are computers that people can use, both patrons and guests. There are even technology rooms for people to learn the latest technologies, such as laser cutting and 3D printing.

She had heard that the original main branch library was a sight to see, but that now it is a federal building, so going in just to wander might not be the best idea. Maggie pads silently through the library and up to the Heritage Room. Her shoes make no noise over the carpeted floor or along the wide steps that she takes to the second floor.

Reaching the heavy doors, she walks into the Heritage Room. "Good Morning, what can we do for you today, Maggie?" The woman sitting at the heavy desk asks. She is a spry senior citizen with salt-and-pepper gray hair that has been cut in a stylish bob. She wears a grey-blue sweater over a white shirt with a black skirt. She looks relatable.

"Hi, Linda. I'm looking for disappearances or murders from 1970 until 2000," Maggie smiles at the woman as she addressed her. She has gotten to know the people in the Heritage Room by name while she had researched the house's previous owners. There are not many people who work in the Heritage Room, so it is not that big of a challenge.

"That's an ambitious undertaking," Linda says, sitting back into her chair. "I have to ask, why are you looking all of this up? There seems to be a bit more to it than simple curiosity."

That's right, I told them that I was just curious, last time. Maggie thought to herself. Nodding, she tells Linda the truth, "Truth be told, I think we have a ghost in the house. I am hoping to figure out who it is, and then maybe the ghost will move on. So far we have had a lot of activity, but no real clues as to who the ghost might be."

"You think you have a ghost?" Linda says. She sounded incredulous.

"Yes, a ghost. We have found cabinets opened, rocking chairs moving, lights turning on and off on their own, light bulbs unscrewing, and a few other things. I know it sounds funny, but I swear, I'm either living in a haunted house, or I'm losing my mind. I'd rather it be the first." Maggie ends her explanation with a giggle. That did not help her appear sane.

"Well, no matter the reasoning, we're here to help. There is a lot of information available, and thirty years' worth of murders alone will take time. Then, if you don't find anything, we can move on to missing persons. Then, if all that fails, we'll see if we can find anything on exorcising ghosts," Linda replies. She has heard a lot of things over the years of working in the library, ghosts are not even in the top five. She would help the woman.

Linda sets Maggie up in her own cubical. There is an old microtape reader that she can use to read the old newspapers. They no longer keep the original papers, they were simply too fragile. Starting in January of 1970, Maggie begins reading the old newspapers, looking at the headlines for murder and missing persons. By the end of the day, she is halfway done with January. It is going to be a long hunt.

Burnt Toys — 1976

Teddy did not go back to work. He had been fired, this time for drinking on the job. Kitty does not say anything about it. It is more than her life is worth to question Teddy or suggest that he might want to get help. Kitty and Annie are just going to have to deal with him in the living room while they work on Annie's classwork in the kitchen.

Every day, Kitty would wake Annie up at her usual time and they would make breakfast together. They would then work on Annie's classwork. They would break for lunch and play a quiet game together, then it would be back to work. They would stop for the day when it was time for Kitty to make dinner. It is a great routine and Annie managed to learn a lot, quickly. She is a very bright child and now with being able to go at her own pace, she soon outpaced the kids who were in her classes.

This came to a grinding halt with Teddy at home again. Teddy insists on getting up with Kitty and insists on a large breakfast, often lingering at the table well after he ate. He has taken to reading the newspaper at the table, something he has never done before. He did not even like the newspapers before he lost this job, saying that it is full of liberal agendas and crack-pot ideas.

Now, he sits at the table and interrupts Kitty's lessons with Annie by shaking the paper loudly, every time they got a little loud. When he finally would finish, he would go into the living room to watch television. Every time he heard them talking in the kitchen, he would increase the volume of the television. Eventually, the television would be blasting and the lesson would have to stop because they would not be able to hear themselves over the television.

Eventually, Kitty tries to salvage the lessons by moving them up to Annie's room. Annie has a desk in her room for her to do her homework. Kitty and Annie can use Annie's bed as a study place and if they need more room, there is always the floor. Teddy being home is not going to stall Annie's education.

One of the things that Kitty thought would be fun for Annie to do would be to put on a play. Kitty knew that Annie was the only student, which meant that Annie would have to use her toys as characters. Annie used to do this when she was a child, so she knows how to do it.

Annie wrote up a script, made set scenes, and practiced. Finally, it is the day of the play. Teddy and Kitty are the audience. Teddy is already drunk, but both Kitty and Annie have gotten used to seeing him that way. He is more often drunk than sober. He is unpleasant in both cases.

Annie is so proud of herself. She wrote a play describing a princess and her hunt for her very own dragon. She uses rollers to change the backgrounds and changes the scenes regularly. It is a very good, fifteen-minute play, for a nine-year-old to develop on her own. She is proud of it. Kitty is proud of her. Teddy is furious.

"This is what you two have been doing up there, every day? Playing with toys?!" He bellows after the play.

"Teddy, Annie made..." Kitty tries to intercede for her daughter.

"I don't care what she made. You two have been wasting time playing with toys, and now you've wasted my time!" He interrupts, screaming down at Kitty who still sits on the couch, where she watched the play. Annie holds perfectly still in front of both of them. She is hoping that Teddy would forget that she is even there.

"Teddy, this is part..." Once again Kitty tries to explain.

"I don't fucking care!" Teddy bellows. He grabbed Annie's toys and crosses into the dining room. He threw them into the fireplace, screaming the entire time. "Annie is nine-years-old. She needs to put down these silly toys and learn her classwork. She needs to learn how to cook, clean, and do her numbers. That's what she needs to be doing!"

He storms into the kitchen, coming back a moment later with lighter fluid and a pack of matches. "You waste my time again, it won't just be toys in this fireplace!" he warns as he douses the toys and sets them ablaze. Kitty grabs Annie as she dashes forward, hoping to save at least some of her toys.

Annie does not scream. She does not sob. She just stands after her Mom grabs her and cries silently, watching her toys melt into black smoky clouds. She stands there and watches her toys burn until they were nothing but black puddles at the bottom of the fireplace. She is just glad that Dolly is not in the group. She has purposefully left Dolly out of the play, just in case something happened to any of the toys. She did not foresee this happening though.

Once her Dad leaves the room, she goes upstairs. There, alone in the dark, she cries. She holds tight to Dolly, crying her sorrow into the soft toy's belly. She knows that she can talk to Mom about her heartbreak, but she is not sure that Mom would not talk to Dad about it. You never know how he will respond. Mom had been very confident that Dad would like her play.

Kitty does not visit Annie that night. She left her daughter alone to deal with her grief. Kitty has her own grief to deal with. She is certain that she and Annie are going to need to get out of the relationship, she just is not sure how. She just knows that this relationship is at an end. She can not have Teddy hurting Annie like this. He cannot keep hurting Kitty like this. It is too much. It is time for all of this to end.

A Light in the Fireplace — 2008

Maggie and Peter are relaxing in the living room. Peter is scrolling through his phone. Maggie is reading her book, Iron Kissed by Patricia Briggs. Peter has a soda at hand, and Maggie has her coffee within reach. She and River are both under the covers, staying warm on this winter night. It is a great way to unwind after a long day at work. It is just a typical Tuesday for them.

It starts with a slight noise, almost like the sound of static, by the fireplace. Peter almost misses the noise completely. He only notices the sound because River and Maggie both turned to the fireplace. He turns around just in time to feel a blast of heat wash over him. It feels like there is a fire going in the old fireplace. He can almost see flames.

The fireplace is decorative. At one time, a very long time ago by the looks of it, it was a functional fireplace. At some point during the home's remodeling, the fireplace was made decorative. The flue is still there, but the fireplace is now too shallow to really use. There are fake logs in it. The gas line has been capped. It can not just light up. It can not produce fire. It looks like there is fire though.

The heat is accompanied by the rancid smell of melted plastic. There are even what appeared to be sparks coming from the fireplace. No one moves during the minute that this took place. As the heat dissipates, Maggie turns to look over at Peter, her face bleached of all color.

"What was that?" Maggie whispers to Peter.

"Um... gas leak?" Peter still denies the ghost, at least out loud.

"Should we call the fire department?"

"Is that what we're supposed to do for a gas leak?"

"Yes. I think so."

"Okay, get dressed. We'll call the fire department and see what they want us to do," Peter agrees, standing up and getting ready to put on something more than his sweats. Maggie stands up with him, looking up the fire department's phone number while she walks upstairs to put on some clothes. River stays under the blankets. It is going to take more than a ghostly fire to get her to go outside and into the cold.

It turns out that all Maggie has to do is call 9-1-1 and the gas company would immediately come out and investigate for a gas leak. They are advised to stand outside of the house and wait for the all-clear. It is a cold night out, but they all have heavy winter coats on, even River, so it could have been worse.

It does not take long for the gas company to make sure that the house does not have a gas leak. They investigate every room, paying special attention to the fireplace, where the Reeds are certain that they smelled gas and that the heat comes from a fire. While the gas company personnel could not explain what happened, they could say with confidence that it was not a gas leak.

Once Maggie and Peter have the all-clear to return inside the home, they stand there, looking at the fireplace. The smell of burnt plastic is gone. There is no indication that anything had happened at all. They can almost believe that it all happened in their head, except that they both had witnessed it. They can remember the heat. They remember the stench. They saw the embers. Something happened, they just can not be sure what that something is.

"Maggie, you might be onto something about this ghost stuff," Peter finally admits.

"Maybe," Maggie is not happy to win this argument. It means that there is a ghost in the house.

"I'll start coming with you on Saturdays to help find some type of information on who this ghost might be. With both of us working on it, it should not take too long," Peter offers.

"If you want to, the help would be appreciated," Maggie smiles. Peter working in the library with her would be great. She can picture it now, them in side-by-side cubicles, pouring over the microfilm, discussing what they find.

"Did that bump in the basement ever go away?" Maggie asks after a moment of them staring at the empty fireplace.

"No. I need to work on that this weekend. I plan on breaking up the cement with a hammer. If I don't find anything, I'll refill it with cement. If I do find something, depending on what it is, we'll have to go from there. I don't want to commit to anything until I know what is down there," Peter answers, leaning up against the back of the couch.

Maggie continues to stand there for a minute, looking at the fireplace. She nods to herself and then turns to Peter. "Okay, I'm going to bed. This has been a less-than-relaxing night. I think I'm going to call it. Hopefully, nothing weird happens while we're sleeping," Maggie laughs quietly. She is completely freaked out by the fireplace incident.

"I'll be up in a minute. Take River with you. She looks tired," Peter says, giving Maggie a quick kiss. He pats her butt as she turns away from him, waving to River to follow her. He pats River's butt as she passes just to be fair. It makes him smile watching them go up the stairs.

Once they were up the stairs, the smile drops from Peter's face. He wants to check the fireplace out better, but he does not want to scare Maggie. He thinks he saw something on the bottom of the fireplace that was not previously there. Now that she is upstairs, he can investigate it without concern.

Peter crosses over to the fireplace and squats down. He is right, something is there. Pulling out his phone, he activates the flashlight feature on it so that he can get a better look. There is a black residue on the bottom of the fireplace. He knew it was not there before. He had remarked as to how clean the fireplace was when they bought the house. It could not have gotten dirty that fast and not with the oily substance he is now fingering. No, whatever this is, it was from the ghostly fire that they experienced.

Dad Gets Mad — 1976

nnie is playing in her room on a fine Saturday evening. She did not have class today with her Mom, instead, she spent the day playing by herself. Mom had gone grocery shopping and even picked her up a small piece of candy that she was saving as an after-dinner snack. Dad spent the day watching college football. Annie can hear him downstairs yelling at the players as though they could hear him.

Annie never understood football. Bobby tried to teach it to her once, but since there were only the two of them, it quickly just became a game of catch and chase. Not that Annie minded that, she had fun with Bobby. She misses playing with Bobby. Since that is out of the question, she has to come up with something else to do for the next hour before dinner is ready. She will color.

Annie has an extensive collection of crayons. Kitty had gotten her the 64 box of Crayola crayons for Christmas. She also had gotten a bunch of coloring books and blank sketch pads. It is one of those coloring books that she is going to use now. The Story Time coloring book is on top of her pile of coloring books because it was her favorite. Flipping to a fresh page, she begins to color.

As she lay there, on the floor, coloring, it was not long before she needs the color black. She uses it all the time. She uses it for shading, to draw shadows, and in the people's hair. It is her most commonly used crayon. As she hunts for it, she remembers that she had to throw it away, she has used all but a tiny nub of it. She will have to find a black crayon somewhere else. She is pretty sure she saw one downstairs in the junk drawer.

Annie pops up and runs down the stairs. She called out, "Hi Dad," as she passes him. She calls hello to her Mom as she runs into the kitchen. When she just ran past Dad, she runs up to her Mom begging for a bite of the food. Kitty has some pasta done and pops a piece in Annie's mouth just as though she were a baby bird. It makes them both smile as Annie quickly chews and swallows the little piece. Then Annie is off again, looking for the black crayon she saw.

Annie opens the junk drawer carefully. She knows it was full of stuff and she does not want to end up with everything falling out of the drawer. That happened once to her and it took her forever to pick up all the nails that had scattered all over the kitchen. There it is, right against the front of the drawer, the black crayon. It says wax crayon, not Crayola, but it is still a crayon.

Annie spins on her toes, and takes off once again, this time to her room. When she gets up there, she carefully sharpens the crayon using the built-in crayon sharpener on her box of crayons and begins to color. A little less than an hour later, her Dad comes up to get her for dinner. That's when he notices the crayon she was using.

The wax crayon that Annie had found was not any old crayon, it is a wax marking crayon. It is one of her Dad's tools that he uses to mark where he was going to make a cut on wood, drywall, or metal. It is specially formulated not to melt and to write on just about everything. Never mind that Teddy has not used it for years, it is his, and he needs it. This little girl just wasted one of his tools on her silly art projects.

The alcohol raises his temper, pushing him to act. He knows his rage was out of proportion to what has happened. It is a crayon for God's sake and she is a kid. At that moment though, it does not matter to him and the drink. He grabs Annie roughly by the back of her shirt, tearing it along the back and ripping out some of her hair. "Where did you get this?" He screams into her face, pointing at the scattered mess that are Annie's coloring supplies.

"The... the crayon?" Annie stammers. She is terribly afraid and a little shocked by the sudden violence.

"Yes, the crayon. The Marking Crayon I use for work," Teddy snears condescendingly.

"I found it in the junk drawer," Annie all but whispers. She is trembling in her fear, but she knows better than to run or fight. If she ran, he would chase her, and it would be far worse.

"That was not junk, but it is now," Teddy snarls, smacking Annie across the face. She hits the bookshelf next to her when he did that and simply sits there, where she lands, face to the shelf. She knows that nothing she said would make it better. It never works for her Mom, why would it work for her?

"You stay here and think on what you did. There will be no dinner for you," Teddy says after a moment a standing there, staring down at the small girl that he is supposed to protect, but is terrifying instead.

Annie stays where she is for a few minutes after Teddy leaves her room. She is hungry, but she has missed dinners before. She still has the candy that her Mom gave her. She will be okay. She changes out of her shirt and jeans and into her pajamas, intent on going to bed early.

Much later that night, after Teddy had passed out, Kitty creeps into Annie's room. She has with her a hot plate of food. She lightly taps on Annie's shoulders to wake her, motioning her to be quiet as she wakes.

Annie takes the plate of food, grateful despite the late hour. She quickly eats the meal while her mother watches her, heartbroken that this is what their lives has come to. As Kitty is leaving, Annie hands her the shirt that she had been wearing. It is destroyed. The tear down the back nearly split the shirt completely. There is nothing that Kitty can do to salvage it. When she takes the plate downstairs to wash it and hide the evidence that she had fed Annie, she throws the shirt away. There is no sense in hanging onto the piece.

Clothes from an Era — 2008

Peter is in the basement, doing his best to break cement. Because the ceiling is so low, he can not actually swing the hammer over his shoulder. Instead, he has to swing the hammer using short strokes, right in front of him. It is loud and messy work. He would much have rather have been at the library with Maggie.

He stops for a moment and looked around. He had gotten up with Maggie earlier that day, excited for what the day was going to bring. They had breakfast together and even though it was still early spring, they managed to get a walk with River. Then Maggie decided it was time for her to go to the library, and work on trying to find out who the ghost might possibly be. Peter had almost gone with her.

Instead, he decided that he would be of more use in solving this mystery, here, in the basement. He had to start and stop a couple of times, but he seems to be in his zone now. The first attempt at this was aborted because River had wanted to help. There were many things that River was good at but since she is a dog, swinging a hammer is not one of them. He had to block off the basement to prevent her from accidentally getting hit by the hammer.

The second attempt was thwarted when the dust from the cement tried to overtake him. He had to stop, and get a mask and a fan. Now he is running a couple of fans, pushing the dust out the side door of the house, while wearing a mask and goggles to protect himself. This is getting to be more of an adventure than he had initially thought it was going to be. And it is a lot hotter than he expected.

Peter eyes his progress. He has been working at this for over an hour, and the cement is finally beginning to give way. Taking an old broom, he sweeps the top of the bump clear of dust and debris. He can clearly see that more cracks are prevalent. He still has a long way to go.

An hour after that, and a couple of breaks in that hour, Peter finally breaks through the cement. How anything could have pushed the floor up with how sturdy that cement was, is beyond him. Considering he has not had water flowing from between the cracks, he figures that it is not water that caused the bump. Maybe tree roots? Those things can be crazy strong and do random things at random times.

People think that trees are slow-growing, slow-moving things. Peter knows better. He had seen what happened when someone buried a bone next to a tree and left it for a week. Roots had grown right through the bone, splitting it. His parents had a tree lift the sidewalk in front of their house in a matter of days. It was flat and smooth, then suddenly buckled and warped with no previous warning. His parents had to replace the entire stretch of the walkway.

Finally, Peter is able to pull off large chunks of cement from the bump. What he finds brings him to a sudden stop. It is a plastic trash bag. It does not have the shape of a person, which is good. But a trash bag, buried under the basement floor, does not bode well for anything.

He considers waiting for Maggie to get home before opening the bag. This might be one of those things that they should discover together. Then he stops and thinks about it again. If it is a body, then there is no way he would want Maggie to see it. It would give him nightmares, and give her traumatic night terrors. She is always jumpier than him. Protecting her from that was more important than doing something together.

Peter goes upstairs to get something to drink, wash his face and hands, and find some rubber gloves. Whatever he is going to find, he is certain that he does not want it on his skin. River is excited to see him, as always, and she tries her best to rush down the stairs to see what Peter has been up to, but with the side door open and a mess in the basement, he does not let her pass. Instead, he lets her outside in the backyard.

The only rubber gloves that Peter can find were the ones that Maggie uses when she has to wash dishes. It is not a chore she does often. She does most of the cooking in the house, which meant that Peter does most of the dishes. The gloves are a little tight, but they are far better than the nothing he was worried he was going to have to use. Grabbing a box cutter, he descends the stairs, once again.

Peter put his mask back on and reaches for the bag. It is surprisingly heavy. With a couple of quick motions, he slices the bag open. He pulls the edges apart, revealing nothing but 1970s-style children's clothes. The clothes appear to have belonged to a girl. They are almost all bright pink and baby blue, where they are not black with age and dirt.

He rummages through the bag for a bit, making sure it does not hold any nasty surprises, like the clothes owner, under them, and then leaves the basement to wash up and call Maggie. She will want to know that he has finally broken through the bump and what he found. She might be irritated at first that he didn't wait for her, but she will understand, especially once she sees it.

***

A couple of hours after Peter called Maggie to tell her what he found, they stand together by the hole that was now their basement floor. "Should we call someone?" Maggie asks Peter, still staring down at the bag of clothes.

"And say what? That we found old clothes buried in the basement?" Peter asks her. While the words are condescending, his tone is gentle.

"Um, yeah. It might be a clue to an old murder that the police have been looking for," Maggie suggests.

"Or it could be the clothes that a child outgrew but they didn't want to throw away. Some people are like that. Or it might be the clothes of a child that passed away due to something like cancer and they couldn't bare to throw her clothes away, so they buried it. No, we shouldn't waste the police's time with something like this. We'll put them in a tote, and then fill the hole. If anyone needs them later, we'll have them," Peter reasons. He has put a lot of thought into what to do with the clothes. He knew that Maggie would agree with him. They would hang onto the clothes for a year and then get rid of them if no use for them comes to light.

"Okay, that sounds like a plan," Maggie agrees.

Hiding Outside — 1976

Maggie is so excited! Bobby came over to play! He has not forgotten about her. That's what they are doing right now, playing. Teddy has finally found another job. This time he promises Kitty that he would stay off the "sauce" and play it straight. She has laid an ultimatum at his feet after he ripped Maggie's shirt. He has to find a job and quit drinking, or they are gone.

Maggie is proud of her Mom for standing up to Dad, but she is not so sure that Mom will keep her word and leave if Dad continues to drink. Maybe if he loses his job again, she might, but Dad has been drinking for as long as Maggie could remember, so she doubts that will change at all.

Right now though, all she is thinking about is playing hide and seek outside with Bobby. She hears him going into the garage, checking behind the shelves in there, looking to see if she is there. She isn't. She is hiding between the garage and the wall that separates her property and the neighbors behind her. They have a heavy, thick cement wall. It reminds Annie of the walled cities that are in some of her books.

While she waits for Bobby to find her, she explores the area a bit. It is a tight fit, even for someone as scrawny as Annie. There are all kinds of things that had fallen between the crack of the two walls. It is mostly leaves and branches from the neighbor's tree, but there are also bottles and papers. Surprisingly, there is also chalk.

These are thick pieces of colored chalk, the ones that are perfect for drawing on cement walls or driveways. It takes a little bit of digging, but she is able to find five big pieces of chalk, all of them in bright colors. She ends up with a red, blue, yellow, green, and white. She has completely forgotten that she was supposed to be hiding, so when she turns around, she finds Bobby staring at her.

"What are you doing?" he asks her, as he backs away from the entrance of the narrow way that she is in.

"I found chalk!" Annie proudly announces, showing him the brightly colored pieces.

"That's cool! Maybe we could draw something on the driveway," Bobby suggests, both of them now forgetting about hide and seek.

Playing with the chalk is a lot of fun for the pair. They draw life-size outlines of each other, filling those outlines in with funny faces and outfits. They draw pictures and use the chalk to play games like hopscotch. For a free toy that Annie found in what was essentially a trash heap, the chalk is one of the best toys that they had played with all day.

As the day wears on, the mosquitoes come out to feast. Not wanting to end their day, they go into the garage to continue writing and drawing. It is dark in there. The garage does not have any electricity. Luckily for them, there are a couple of windows in the garage, and they leave the door open, giving them just enough light to play tick-tack-toe. Bobby leaves as the sun began to set, leaving Annie to continue to draw in the garage, alone.

Playing with the chalk is more fun when Bobby is around. She is glad that he had gotten a chance to come over and visit her. She was afraid that he had forgotten her, between classes, sports, and his new friends. It is nice to know that someone likes her besides her Mom. Now that he was gone, she could not play tick-tack-toe anymore, but she could still draw.

Annie draws flowers and hearts on the garage wall. She wants to put her and Bobby's initials in some of the hearts, but she does not want Dad to know about Bobby. She also is not sure that Bobby likes her as she likes him. She does not want him to go away because he thinks it is gross that a girl might like him. Instead, she just fills the hearts in, knowing what she would put in them if she could.

As it continues to get dark, Annie is forced to leave the garage. She can barely see her hand in front of her face. She goes back to the driveway, where she can see her hopscotch board. The mosquitoes have quit being so prevalent, and the lightning bugs are beginning to come out. She plays there until it was time to come in for dinner.

Dinner is quiet. Dad had not gotten drunk on his way home, but Annie could smell the beer on him, meaning that he had stopped and had a drink before coming home. At least he is not drunk. Annie can be happy about that, and it looks like Kitty is happy. Annie is most happy about Kitty being happy.

As Kitty and Annie clean up after dinner, Annie asks, "Can I have a mason jar and collect lightning bugs?" Annie had seen a picture of a jar of lightning bugs in one of her books. It looks like fun to collect the bugs, and then they could light up her room.

"Sure," Kitty answers her with a smile. She crosses over to the pantry and grabs one of the large jars with a metal ring on it. "We'll have to use a paper towel as a lid, otherwise the lightning bugs won't be able to breathe and they'll die." Kitty shows Annie how to secure the paper towel under the metal ring, making for a loose but breathable lid. Then she turns the child out into the yard to collect lightning bugs.

Annie chases lightning bugs up and down her yard, catching them and then depositing them in the mason jar. She had put down some grass and sticks in the jar, making a small habitat for the little bugs. After an hour, Kitty calls her in and smiles as Annie shows her the jar and her collection of bugs.

"Okay, you can keep them for tonight. Tomorrow morning though, you're gonna have to let them go. It is only fair to them. You wouldn't want someone to keep you in a jar forever, would you?" Kitty asks Annie as they get ready for bed.

"I guess you're right. Tomorrow morning, I'll let them go. But for tonight, can they stay on my bedside table? I want to watch them as I fall asleep," Annie answers her.

"Sure thing, kiddo."

Annie slept the sleep of a happy child that night, content to dream of chalk drawings and lightning bugs in jars.

Writing on the Walls — 2008

There is little in the world as great as coming home from a long day at work. For Peter and Maggie, it is even better because the first people they see after work are each other. Then they go and get River to take her for a walk. It is as pleasant of a way to end what could easily be a trying day. Since Maggie and Peter work the same shift, they take turns driving to work, with one dropping the other off. The person who drops the person off is then the person to pick up their partner. Today it is Maggie's turn to do the drop-off, pick-up routine.

When she had left for work with Peter, she had a very clear look at the inside-back of the garage. She had even had a thought that stuck in her mind about how the ivy was beginning to grow between the roof and the wall of the garage and that they were going to have to do something about that before it tore down the garage. Ivy can be very detrimental to structures if it is allowed to grow unchecked. The wall itself is clean and clear though, with no cracks, no writing. It is just a blank wall.

When Maggie pulls into the garage, she is startled to find chalk drawings all over the back of the garage. She is so startled, that she hit the brakes a little too hard causing Peter to be jolted forward in his seat, hitting against his seat belt. As he stares at her in disbelief and incomprehension, he notices the look of startlement on Maggie's face. Following her gaze, he, too, is shocked to find the garage had been decorated while they were gone.

Maggie puts the car in park and turned it off, half sticking out the garage. Together, Peter and she go to investigate the chalk drawings. What they find is rather sweet. There were games of tick-tack-toe. Some of the O's were drawn as hearts. There are also flowers, hearts, and stars drawn and colored in around the games. The drawings could not have been placed there recently, they are behind some of the shelves and equipment that Maggie and Peter stored in the garage.

"These look like they have been here for a long time," Peter says, as he looks at a pretty pink flower. It has a yellow center and blue highlights.

"I know I looked at the back of the garage today and I know I didn't see these then," Maggie answers him. She is looking at a Tic-tac-toe game that had ended in a stalemate.

"I haven't noticed them before, either. More ghost activity?" Peter guesses.

"I am going to assume so. How else would someone get in and draw all over the wall without knocking down any shelves? If it has been neighborhood children, wouldn't they draw on the outside or at least on one of the clear walls?"

"Yeah, that's what I thought, too," Peter agrees with a sigh.

"This does tell us something about our ghost though," Maggie says, trying to find the bright side to the sudden artwork.

"Yeah?"

"This tells us that the ghost is a young girl. Not quite a teenager, from the height and the composition of the drawings."

"How do you figure?" Peter asks, looking over at his wife. Maggie was still looking at the drawings. This one was a heart with a yellow highlight on it.

"Well, how many young boys do you know that draw hearts and flowers? Not saying they couldn't, but most don't, at least in my experience. The kid has to be pre-teen or younger, either that or very short because the drawings come to my chest and most people draw at face level," Maggie reasons.

Peter mimes drawing on the wall, raising his hand as though he had chalk. He has to agree, it was far more comfortable to draw at face level than chest level. "Okay, that will help us in narrowing down our search, I think. You are planning on going to the library this Saturday, right?"

"Yeah, I think we have to. No matter what caused this ghost to stick around, I don't think they're going to move on until we figure out who they are or complete whatever task they need to be done," Maggie says, turning away from the drawing.

"Are we going to leave these drawings up, or do you want me to bring the hose back and wash them off?" Peter asks, not bothering to get back in the car with Maggie.

"I think we can leave them. They're not hurting anything," Maggie answers after she rolls the window down. Maggie put the car in drive again and parked it where it normally went. She could almost make out initials in the heart, but they were not clear enough for her to see, maybe one set was an AK, but she was not sure. Whoever made the heart had made a point to cover up the initials as well as could be.

Maggie and Peter take a look around the rest of the garage. They could not find anything that was out of place or any other marks that would possibly indicate that anyone had been in the garage. It is as though those images just appeared, which, with how all of the rest of the things in the house just randomly happen, this does not surprise the couple.

"Whoever did that artwork seemed to have a sweet heart," Peter says as they walk into their house through the back door. The front door is for visitors, the backdoor is for family.

"What do you mean?" Maggie asks him.

"Well, of all the things that they could have drawn, they drew flowers and hearts. Those are sweet things, friendly things. This is a ghost we're dealing with. They could have drawn terrifying images and it would have fit," Peter reasons.

"I think I agree with you. Whoever this ghost is, they are definitely sweet. If you think about it, they could have done some really mean things, but they only do small pranks and are sometimes even helpful. Like the time the ghost turned on the light for me because I was too lazy to do it myself. That's not a mean spirit, it's a friendly, almost helpful one," Maggie smiles to herself, remembering the almost scary event in a much better light now that it was past.

"That kind of makes me want to find who this person was even more. I would hate to think of a sweet child stuck in some type of endless limbo. They deserve to be happy in the afterlife," Peter says, planting a kiss on the top of Maggie's head. Together they harness up River and take her for her walk. There is nothing more they can do that day.

The Final Accident — 1976

Dinner has finished in silence. It is a month after Kitty's ultimatum with Teddy, and he has been doing better, until this night. He is drunk, again. He is not violent, not yet anyway. He is just sullen, staring at the table through dinner, barely eating. Where there had been some discussion at the dinner table most days, and often a lively discussion on the weekends, tonight's dinner's only words were for the salt.

Teddy stays seated in his spot as Annie and Kitty begin to clear the table. It is almost as though he is oblivious to what is going on around him. It is not normal for Teddy in any situation. Kitty and Annie do their best to be as quiet as possible as they work around him. That fails miserably when Annie drops a plate.

Kitty has been doing the dishes, leaving it to Annie to dry the dishes before putting them in their respective cabinets. The cabinet that the plates go in was a little too tall, but Annie figures she could reach it. She has managed to get the plates in the cabinet before. It also happens to be right next to Teddy.

Annie has managed to get the plates up to the shelf in the cabinet on her own. She is just pushing them in when one of them slipped from the top of the stack. She tries to catch it, fumbling all of them in the process. The crash of the fallen plates is nearly deafening as they hit the counter below the cabinet and then the floor. It is not half as deafening as what happens next.

Kitty always knew that Teddy's temper would be his downfall. After years of being married to him, and seeing how he is getting worse, she fears it might be the downfall of their whole family. She just never imagined that the offense would be so great.

Kitty spins around at the sound of the plates hitting the floor. She watches as it is Annie who hits the floor next. Teddy is looming over her, flatware shattered at his feet. There is no blood surrounding her, but Kitty knows in her heart of hearts that Annie is dead.

Kitty dives for Annie, pulling her into her arms, heedless of the glass that digs into her knees. Her daughter, once so full of life, is limp in her arms. Her head rolls, her neck broken. It had snapped as it hit the countertop. She was dead before she even hit the floor. It is no consolation to her mother who felt her heart shatter. It takes Teddy a bit longer to realize what happened.

Watching his wife keen over their dead daughter, Teddy knows that this is not something he would be able to ever fix. He has murdered the one thing in his life that was worth anything, and he did it because he could not control himself. Kitty had warned him that he would lose everything if he did not straighten up. He just never thought it would be like this.

Teddy collapses, head in his hands, tears flowing. He knows he should reach out and comfort Kitty. He just does not know how. He knows that he should try to comfort Annie, after all, he hurt her, but he also knows she is beyond any comfort that he might offer. He had done some horrible things in Vietnam, but he has never done anything that came close to this. This was the worst thing he could have ever done.

The tears flow in that kitchen for most of the night. Once Kitty had cried herself nearly to sleep, still clutching her daughter, she decides she was going to need help. "I have to call 9-1-1," she says to herself. Unfortunately, she says it aloud.

Hearing his wife say words, and have those words being that she was going to call someone is enough to snap Teddy out of his self-pitying stupor. "We can't do that."

Kitty turns to him with a look of incredulity, "What do you mean? Our daughter is dead. We need to call someone." The wrongness of his statement is enough to stop her tears for the moment.

"No. We can take care of this ourselves. We'll bury her ourselves. If we call people, they'll arrest us both, and we'll both be charged with murder. No, we can just handle this," Teddy's voice becomes clearer as he speaks. He sounded calm and confident.

"HA! No, they will just arrest you. You killed our daughter! If you think I'm letting you get away with this, you're out of your fucking mind!" Kitty screams as she lunges for the phone. It is in the living room, and she has to pass Teddy to get to it. She does not make it.

Teddy grabs her as she tries to pass him. He holds her down as she fights him to get free. He covers her mouth to muffle her screams. When her fight gets to be too much for him, he slowly chokes her. He is not going to jail this night.

Once Kitty is unconscious, he carries her to the bathroom upstairs and locks her in. He will take care of Annie. Kitty will be fine for a few days in the bathroom. It has water. He will even come by and feed her, making sure she does not starve. Of all the rooms to be locked in, the bathroom is the best one. It has the added benefit of being the only room in the house without a window.

The first thing Teddy figures he will have to do is get rid of Annie's body. He considers where he could put her. Burying her in the backyard is not an option. It is too exposed. Burying her in the basement might work. As he paces the front room, he looks out the front windows. The street was dark and all is quiet. While his house might be on the verge of chaos, the rest of the world is peaceful. That was when he sees the answer to his dilemma. He knows where he going to put Annie. He also knows how he was going to disguise her smell.

The next issue, after stashing Annie, is what to do with her stuff. He is going to make it look like she had never existed, or at least like she moved with them when they move later this week. He needs to, otherwise, people would wonder what happened to the child that the clothes belongs to. That he decides will go in the basement. He will bury the clothes there. Clothes do not stink. Toys are easy to get rid of, he would just dump them off at the Salvation Army, claiming that they are no longer wanted.

By the morning's light, Annie's body is gone, and Teddy is well on his way to erasing her from ever existing. Annie might have been the best thing he ever had a hand in creating, but since he killed her, he is now obligated to eliminate her existence completely. Ignoring Kitty pounding at the bathroom door, he works through the day and night, not stopping in his frenzy.

Fallen Slats — 2008

Maggie, Peter, and River all sit together on the couch. The wind is howling outside. The windows are shaking in their frames, but the house itself is still. It is a late spring storm, and the rain is coming almost sideways. Inside the brick home, it is warm and comfortable. The lights are on, and the blankets are warm. The couch is barely big enough for three, but it makes for a comfortable cuddle session.

When the power goes out, Peter and Maggie feign a gasp of fear, but in reality, they are just playing. They feel safe and comfortable in their home, even knowing that it is most likely haunted. The ghost is simply not always on their mind. With months between events, it is easy to forget about the haunting.

Maggie gets up after a couple of minutes of sitting in the dark with Peter and River and gathers some candles. Lighting them, the candles bring a sense of warmth to the already warm home. It is almost idyllic, especially since they do have to go to work in the morning.

Eventually, they decide to bed since the power has not come back on. Taking the candles with them, they mount the stairs. That is when they hear it. There are a series of crashes from outside. They feel the ground shake for a moment, even through the foundation of the house. It feels as though it is coming from the front of the home.

Taking care to set the candles down on the end tables first, they peer through the front windows. Through the rain, they can see a large bough of the tree in front of their house has fallen across the sidewalk. That was what caused the crashes that they had heard.

They also see some damage on their porch, a couple of slats on the ceiling of the porch have fallen down in the storm. Both of those problems can wait until the morning though. Picking up the candles once again, they make their way upstairs and to bed.

***

The next morning is a sharp contrast to the night before. Where the night before was dark and stormy, the morning is bright and sunny. It was as though the storm had blown itself out and the sunlight has replaced it. It set the mood for the small family.

They start their day with eggs and toast. Even River gets to enjoy an egg with her kibble. They decide against going for a walk. It was simply too wet outside and River likes rolling in the mud just a little too much. They check the cement repair that Peter had done a couple of months earlier and found that holding. That helps the mood in the house.

Once breakfast is eaten and dishes are done, they decide to address the branch on the sidewalk. Leaving River to play in the yard, Peter and Maggie gather up some supplies, mainly a hatchet and a saw, and go to tackle the branch. Working together, it takes them nearly an hour to cut and pile the branch parts on the side of the road. It is a very big branch.

Maggie peers up at the tree after using the hatchet to cut pieces of wood into more manageable sizes. "It looks like it was almost half of the top of the tree that fell down."

"Yeah, I'm just glad it happened during the storm so that there was no one underneath it when it came down. It could have killed someone," Peter agrees, looking up at the tree as well.

"Good thing it landed on the sidewalk and not in the street. With how it was raining last night, if it had landed in the street, it would have caused an accident for sure. No one would have been able to see it, and I certainly did not want to go out into the rain to get it. Not that we'd have been able to move it," Maggie says, now looking at the pile of wood that they had cut.

"That's the truth. But it is cleared up now. We only have one more thing to fix from last night, but first, lunch. That was hard work clearing that branch," Peter takes Maggie around the shoulders and leading her to the backyard where River waited for them. They drop off their tools in the garage and make lunch.

After lunch, they decide to take care of the downed slats on the porch. They figure it would be an easy fix, just put them back up and secure them with nails. No trouble, no fuss. They are wrong. The slats do not want to just go back up.

The first part of the problem is that they had a hard time reaching the slats. They have a ladder, but even then, the porch ceiling is very high. They have to stand on the next to top step to reach the slats. The next problem is fitting the slats together. They are all tongue and groove slats, meaning that the slats have to fit together to lay flat against the ceiling joists. As Peter fusses with this, he thinks he catches a glimpse of something hiding in the rafters of the ceiling.

"Maggie, could you get me a flashlight?" Peter asks, looking down at Maggie from the top of the ladder.

"Sure. What's up?" Maggie responds before stepping into the house to find a flashlight.

"I think I see something up here. If it is an animal, I don't want to trap them in the ceiling with no way to escape. It would be a horrible death, and they might damage something trying to escape," Peter answers as he peers into the dark. He can almost make it out, but not quite. There is something in there, but he cannot quite tell what it is.

"Oh, I hope it's not an animal. If it hasn't gotten up and moved yet, it might be terrified or injured. If it's injured, we're gonna have to trap it and take it to the vet," Maggie comments before disappearing into the house.

"We are not taking a wild animal to the vet," Peter calls after her. He can only hope it was not a cat. He could see Maggie insisting on taking the cat to the vet, and then deciding that it was their responsibility to care for the creature. Peter does not want to be owned by a cat.

It only takes a moment for Maggie to find the flashlight. It is a large, hefty thing that has a beam like a floodlight. Whatever he is going to be shining that light on would definitely be blinded afterward. Not that it could be helped, they do not own any other type of flashlight. Peter almost drops the flashlight from the shock of what he finds.

"Maggie, call the police. I think I found our ghost."

A Panicked Move — 1976

Teddy is a strong man. He is a capable man. It does not take long for him to open a couple of slats in the ceiling of the porch and slide Annie's body into the rafters there. She was such a tiny thing, after all. He works in the dark of that first night to hide her body. She is so small, she is easy to handle, even when she becomes stiff. With the slats being tongue and grove, he does not even need to nail them into place, just lock them against the before and aft boards. It is simple for him, and with it being so dark outside, no one even notices him.

He makes sure to find some roadkill to put on the porch, making sure that anyone who smells her would assume it is that. He even put a dead raccoon under the porch, near the front of it to detract notice of the small child hidden in the rafters.

Getting rid of her clothes is a little bit more work. It does not take long for Teddy to dig a hole in the basement. It is just a bare packed earth flooring. He puts the heavy, clay-like dirt from the hole he digs, in the backyard again in the dark of night. Without a single light on and wearing his darkest clothes, Teddy is nearly invisible as he moves about the backyard, spreading the buckets of dirt that he has dug up. When he is done, no one would be able to tell that new dirt had been added by the light of the day.

Annie's clothes are easy to gather up. She had been such a neat child, always taking care to put her clothes away. It has only taken a single trash bag to gather her clothes and drop them in the pit that he had dug. A couple bags of cement and a couple of gallons of paint is all that is needed to completely hide the murder of his only child.

Through all of this, Kitty remains locked in the bathroom. She has stopped banging on the door. She has lost her voice from the constant screaming. She is weak from lack of food and the ability to move more than a couple of feet at a time. Now, when he brings her food, she just glares at him, red-rimmed eyes full of hate and anger.

Despite Kitty's fury, Teddy believes that it is something they could get through, together. Sure, killing Annie was a horrible mistake, one that he would take back if he could. But he can't, and he knows it. They will simply have to move on from here. There could be a new Annie in time, one that would not know the angry and drunk Teddy. He could change, and he would change.

It takes two days for Teddy to completely hide that Annie had ever existed. No one has commented about the smell coming from their porch. The basement cement is dry and the floor is painted, hiding the new cement from notice. Now all that is left was to get out of the house and to a new city, one where no one knows their name and has never heard of a little girl called Annie.

Knowing that Kitty would fight him, and fight hard, Teddy withholds her food while he packs their truck with everything it can carry. They would be moving quickly, so they only have their essentials. Everyone would think that they were skipping out on their rent. It would make sense considering they are often behind on the rent. Sure, they are currently caught up, but everyone knows that can change in the blink of an eye. By the time people notice that they are gone, Annie should not even be noticeable.

Using old suitcases, Teddy packs all of Kitty's and his clothes. Like Annie, Kitty is a neat person by nature. All of her clothes are already hanging up or neatly folded. His clothes take more time to pack, but he owns less, so it evens out. He packs their kitchen supplies and food. He packs their bedding. He leaves the photo albums. They will not want those wherever they end up. They are filled with pictures of Annie.

Once everything is packed, it is time to get Kitty. For a second, he seriously considers just leaving her locked in the bathroom. If he just drove away, she would eventually figure out a way to get out of the bathroom, and he would be gone. But, if she escapes, she would call the police and there would be a manhunt on for him. She has to come with him. He has to make sure that she does not call the police. He sets a couple of his belts on the passenger seat, he is going to have to secure her once they are in the car. He goes to go get his wife.

By now, Kitty has gone a day and a half with nothing to eat and nothing to drink but tap water from the sink. She does not even have a cup to drink it from, just her hands. She is weak and tired. When Teddy comes for her, she fights, but she simply does not have the strength to keep up the fight. It does not take much for him to get her into the truck. Once there, he belts her legs together and belts her hands behind her. Buckling her into the front seat, she is not going anywhere. She would have screamed if she had not already broken her voice in her earlier fury.

Teddy hops in the driver's seat, turned on the radio, and drives down the street, seemingly on a pleasant day trip. As the miles roll under their wheels, tears rolls down Kitty's face. Who knew that one body could hold so many tears?

Teddy makes only two stops before they leave town. The first one is to the local ATM to withdraw the last of the money from his banking account. There is not much in the account. Not enough to have covered rent, even if they would have stayed. The next stop is to put gas in the truck. He purposefully chooses a self-serve station, one that is out of the way from mainstream traffic. Using a credit card, he fills the tank. Picking a direction, any direction, he then proceeds to drive away from the life that they had known, leaving Annie behind for good.

The Dark Find — 2008

There is yellow caution tape everywhere, it seems. There is tape in the basement, surrounding the newly dug-up hole. The initial hole has been greatly enlarged, now taking up most of the basement. There are now beams bracing the walls to ensure the foundation does not collapse with the sudden reduction of support that the floor had been providing.

There is tape on the porch, surrounding the entire thing. Maggie and Peter can not use the front door at all. The entire ceiling for the porch has been taken down, plank by plank, looking for clues as to who this person might be and who might have put that person up there.

It is a dark find, to be sure. The body, little more than a dried skeleton, is small. The clothes that hangs from the bones are greatly decomposed, but enough of them remain to indicate that the body belonged to that of a young girl. The remaining hair, blond and long, seems to collaborate with that. The cause of death appears to be a broken neck, but an autopsy would be done to confirm that. What is clear was that whoever this was, they died around the same time that Maggie and Peter were being born. Maggie and Peter could not have been suspects.

The police take the tote of clothes that Peter had found, bag and all. While they wish that the couple would have called the police when they first found the bag, they understand the hesitancy that the couple expressed. They did not want to be responsible for wasted resources and calling the police for some old clothes did sound a little like overkill, right up until you pair it with the body of a child.

While the police are busy taking over their home, Maggie, Peter, and River move into a local hotel. They would only be in the way of any type of search that the police might be doing.

"Do you think they will find who that person was?" Maggie asks Peter, as they lay in the unfamiliar room, on an unfamiliar bed. Sleep is slow coming. She had not seen the body, but she had a vivid imagination and kept picturing a human skull whenever she closes her eyes.

"Of course, they will figure out who the body belonged to, and they will figure out who put them in the ceiling of the porch. I am sure that they will be able to get DNA evidence or something. They have resources that we don't have. It will be easy for them to find out what happened," Peter reassures her. Pulling Maggie into his arms, he smooths her hair, trying to give her some comfort, while taking solace in her arms. He had seen the body, and the image was seared in his brain. He is not sure he would ever be able to get the sight of a decomposed little girl out of his mind.

"Do you think the ghost will go away, now that the body had been found?" Maggie asks quietly.

"I have no idea. I would think so. Why else would the ghost have stuck around, except to make sure that they got to be laid to rest as they deserved?" Peter whispers.

"That's a good point. Are we going to sell the house?" Maggie wonders.

"I don't know. Do you want to sell the house? Are you comfortable living in a house where a dead body was hidden? We lived there for a year already, but that does not mean we have to continue living there. A lot has happened while we have been living there. It might be better to sell it once this is all over. I'm sure someone would want to buy it, if for no other reason than that a body had been found there," Peter answers. He stops and thinks about it for a minute and then continues. "Maybe we should not make any decisions right now. It has been a very trying past few months and we don't want to make any rash decisions that we'll regret later."

"You're right," Maggie agrees, yawning mid-way through. It had been a long and stressful day. It is beginning to catch up with her. River is already asleep, laying across their legs like a fuzzy blanket. It is comforting in the way that only dogs can be comforting.

***

The next morning sees them up early. Their sleep had been deep, despite the gruesome dreams that plagued them both. Sometimes exhaustion trumps everything else. Grabbing River's leash and harness, they set off to find some breakfast. McDonald's is hardly the healthiest of starts to one's day, but their coffee is hot and their food is quick and tasty. River even enjoys a couple of the breakfast sandwiches instead of her normal kibble, which is still at the house.

They are allowed into the house to grab a change of clothes, but then quickly ushered out again. The police are doing their best to secure a crime scene thirty years too late. Dropping River off at Maggie's Mom's house, Peter and Maggie go back to the library. Now they had a better clue as to who they are looking for, they begin to dig once again for a missing girl, sometime in the 1970s.

Peter and Maggie spend the day at the library. They decide that rather than sleeping at the hotel again, they would join River at Maggie's Mom's house. It is not a huge house, but they could sleep on the couch. It is more comfortable than the hotel and its huge, but unknown bed. They need comfort, they need familiarity. Maggie needs her Mom.

When Maggie's Mom, Kathy, found out what they had found in their home, she was quick to insist that they stay with her. She was horrified that anything could have happened to a little child, she had been so protective of Maggie when she was growing up. Maggie's Dad, Mike, had lived in awe of Maggie, insisting that she was the perfect child. Maggie misses him a great deal. She could have used one of his great big bear hugs. It has been 10 years since he passed away.

A Sudden Disappearance — 1976

Bobby is the first one to notice that the Koonz family had moved away. It is a couple of weeks after Teddy had driven himself and Kitty out of the city, with all of their essentials. Bobby wants to play with Annie, so he rings the doorbell. He sees the dead raccoon, stinking and rotting on the porch. He is loath to go near it though. Maggots are feasting on it, crawling and squirming, almost making it look as though it is alive.

He rings the doorbell a couple of times, but the stench is too much for him, and he soon leaves. He finds some of his other friends to play with that day, but he does not forgotten how no one answered the door. There is almost always someone home at the Koonz house.

When he gets the same response the next few times he rings the bell, he finally tells his parents about it. By then the raccoon has quit stinking quite as much. The maggots had done their job and stripped it of most of its meat. All that was left is some skin and bones. It is a gruesome sight, but nothing that a young boy had not seen before, playing out in the bigger parks.

His parents do not say much about the disappearance. They had seen Kitty and Teddy before. They know the type of man that Teddy is. That the family had stayed in that big house for as long as they had was a surprise to them. They do their best to explain to Bobby that sometimes, people just left. It is not Annie's fault that she did not say goodbye, she likely did not even know she was leaving until right before they drove away.

The Landlord, Robin McGuire is the next one to notice that the Koonz family had skipped town. They were behind on their rent. They were frequently behind, and he always let them make it up. This time, their phone is disconnected. He needs the money, or he needs them gone. There is only so much leeway that a man can give another man.

McGuire is disgusted by the dead raccoon that he found on the porch. Stopping first to grab a shovel out of the back of his truck, he gets rid of the mess. It has left a dark stain on the porch where it had decomposed. The stench seems to linger. Ringing the doorbell, he is beginning to get irritated as no one answers the door. By the fifth time he rings and finds no movement inside the house, he fetches his keys and walks in.

At first, it looks like the family had just been out, not vacated. The television and the couches are still there. The artwork on the walls is still there, including some family photos, although some frames are empty. The house is not trashed, just a little messy. The dining room holds no surprises either. The kitchen is what makes McGuire begin to realize that the house was no longer inhabited. There is no food in the refrigerator. The cabinets have some mismatched pieces in them, but they are also mostly empty.

Going upstairs, McGuire finds empty beds, empty dressers, and empty closets. The Koonz family had left in a hurry. It looks like the only family member who got to keep everything but their furniture is the little girl. There are no toys, no photos, and no clothes of hers to be found anywhere in the house.

McGuire is furious. He was going to have to pay people to come in and empty out the house of all the junk that was left in it. He would do what he could to recoup the losses through yard sales and auctions, but he knows he can not get much for what was left. Nothing there is of high quality. Most of it would fall apart before he manages to get it out of the house.

Tenets skipping out on their rent is not uncommon. It happens a lot more frequently than most people believe. Most of the time when they do that, they destroy the home that they are living in. At least the Koonz family did not do that. They just left. McGuire has a "Notice of Belief of Abandonment" in his truck and he attaches it to the front door. The family has fifteen days to call him, or he would begin to empty the house of all of their possessions. Fifteen days is more time than he is required to give, but he was a generous soul.

McGuire does not expect to hear from Teddy or his wife Kitty. He is not surprised when after the fifteen-day mark, no actions have been taken by the tenants. By then, he has moved the utilities back into his name. He does not feel like emptying a house that did not have electricity or heat. At least the smell in front of the house has passed. He would empty, clean, and lease the house to another family. One that might actually pay their rent on time.

The only surprise that McGuire has in the clean-up of the house was in the basement. He is pretty sure that he did not paint the basement floor. He is pretty sure the floor had been packed earth last time he saw it. He sees a lot of basements though. He could not be positive of that though. It looked almost new, but then, maybe the kid had played down there and they kept it clean for her. There is no reason for him to investigate further into that.

He is not surprised when the neighbor boy stopped by to see if he knows where the family had gone. He boy, Bobby, had been friends with the little girl. He is hoping that maybe they could be at least pen pals. It breaks McGuire's heart to have to tell little Bobby that he had no idea where the Koonz family had gone. He might be angry with Teddy, but there is no reason to take it out on a neighbor's child.

On the last night of the clean-up, McGuire goes to his files and makes a note on the financial file marked Koonz and the property address. He stamps it as closed, non-payment. If he came across that family name again, he would know not to rent to them. He would keep those files for a decade, but then he would get rid of them. No one needs files forever.

A Final Rest — 2008

It does not take long for the police to take the child's body away for autopsy. Even though the body has waited decades for discovery, the pathologists are quick to begin their work. They are quickly able to determine that the child was a young, pre-puberty girl. It takes even less time for them to determine the cause of death being a broken neck caused by blunt force trauma.

Since there was no known kin to claim the body, the state is responsible for the burial of the child. Maggie and Peter could not stand for her to be buried alone, so they take custody of the body and make arrangements with the local funeral parlor to have her properly buried in a nice casket.

"She has been alone, shoved in a rafter for too long. She needs to be with people who care that she exists," Maggie tells Peter once she finds out that the state was going to bury her with the rest of the unknown and unclaimed souls. Maggie can not bare it. She does not know the child, but she still feels something of a connection to her.

Peter and she are sitting around her Mother's kitchen table. Kathy is busy making scones, one of her favorite treats. They are still staying at Kathy's home, living on the couch. It is not the most comfortable place to sleep, but it works well enough. They are allowed to go back home, but there is a lot of work that needs to be done to the house to repair what had been damaged during the police investigation. They want the contractors to fix it first, and then they would see how they feel about continuing to live there.

"Funerals are expensive," Peter counters. He feels something of a connection to the child, too. He is just less inclined to take on the responsibility for her body.

"Well, yes. But we would not be doing a viewing. We'd just be buying a casket and a burial plot. It would be a couple of thousand dollars, but still, I feel that she deserves it. If nothing else, it would make me feel better," Maggie says, playing her trump card. If it is for her, she knows that Peter would do anything, even bury an unknown child.

"I'm going to guess that you want to get her a couple of toys to take with her. She has been alone for a very long time. They estimate that she had been up there for thirty years," Peter guesses what his wife is going to want.

"Yes. Maybe a plush toy dog and a baby doll like the one that we found on our backstep all those months ago," Maggie answers. She had thought about it before broaching the topic with Peter.

"Fine. We'll call the coroner's office tomorrow morning. They should be able to release the body to us or direct us to someone who can help us. Is the funeral home around the corner the one you want to go with?"

"Yeah, that one is fine. I've been there before. I'm sure that they will be able to give her the attention that she needs."

"Why don't we swing by there tomorrow," Kathy suggests as she put her scones in the oven.

"Okay, we can do that. We'll stop and pick up some toys for her on the way there," Maggie agrees. Peter just nods. He knew from the start that he was not going to win this battle. Good thing that they have some savings put away.

The following day, the three of them go to Autumn Falls Funeral Home to look at caskets. It is a local funeral home, right around the corner from Peter and Maggie's home. With Kathy in tow, they look at the various caskets that are available. The children's ones were the most heartbreaking of the lot, but that is what they needed.

In the end, they decide to buy a pale pink casket, lined with white velvet. They know that no one is going to see it, but they feel that it is something she deserves in death because life had not been kind to the kid. Kathy insists on paying for the casket, leaving Peter and Maggie to buy the plot and vault. They decide to buy not only that plot, but the ones next to it, ensuring their final resting places are near the child that they never met. She might have been forgotten in life, but she would not be forgotten in death.

They do not get a gravestone for her though. Instead, they decide on the simple metal plaque that the cemetery provides. If they ever determine who she was, then they could add a stone later. With all of that, it was nearly $5,000, split between Maggie and Peter, and Kathy. Maggie feels that it was worth it, putting the child's body to rest. She can only hope that it would put the ghost to rest as well.

It is a foggy morning, unseasonably chilly as they watch the casket being lowered into the ground. It is such a little casket, cradling a tiny body. Maggie had not seen them put the toys in the casket with the child, but she trusted that they were there. She could not bare to look upon the body. She knows it would haunt her nightmares forever if she did.

Maggie, Peter, Kathy, and the Funeral Director from Autumn Fall are the only ones in attendance. After she is laid to rest, the Funeral Director leaves, leaving Maggie, Peter, and Kathy alone in the cemetery. Together they wander through the lot, looking at the somber and meditative scenery before them. The lots themselves are on a hill, overlooking a small lake. There are trees behind them, but not close enough that their roots would bother the dead. Flowers are everywhere. It is a peaceful place.

"Have you two decided what you're going to do with your house?" Kathy asks them as they gazed at the lake.

"I think I'll try to live in it. We lived there for almost a year before we discovered her. There is no reason we could not continue to live there," Maggie answers for the two of them. Peter does not look surprised. Maggie loves that house.

"Okay. If you decided you don't like it, you guys can come back and live with me while you work on selling the house. I really don't mind," Kathy reminds them. She rather likes them living with her. She even likes having River following her around the kitchen, picking up the crumbs that she drops. Her house is too quiet with it just being her there.

"We'll visit," Maggie promises.

"How long until the contractors are done?" Kathy asks.

"They should be done next week," Peter answers.

"We should do something this weekend then since it will be the last weekend you guys will be staying with me," Kathy suggests.

"Okay, your choice. You have helped us so much, so you can decide what you want to do to celebrate," Maggie agrees, smiling over at her Mom and then Peter. The three of them wander over to Peter's car and go back to Kathy's home. They are looking forward to a nice lunch, and then making plans to return to their lives.

The Clean Getaway — 1976

Teddy drives himself and Kitty to Chicago. It is a long trip west from the nowhere town they started from in western Pennsylvania. They pass several large cities along the way, but Teddy does not want to stop at the first or even the second city that they come across. It is too close to people who might know them. It is too close to his crime. It is too close to Annie.

Teddy is not a total monster to Kitty during the drive. He keeps her tied up, but he does stop every few hours at rest stops and lets her use the bathrooms. He makes sure to meet her at the door to the women's bathroom and to only allowed her access to them when the place is empty though. He has to make sure that she does not talk to anyone about Annie's death.

Teddy knows that taking Kitty away from their home as he did was kidnapping. He reasons it away that he is making the best decision for their family. Kitty will agree with him once she calms down, he is sure of it. Besides, it is his right to take his wife to a new city, if she agrees or not. After all, she was *his* responsibility as *his* wife.

He stops for food once, parking the car in the back corner of the fast food joint. He goes in, orders, and hand-feeds Kitty, taking care that she does not bite him. Just because she could not use her hands or feet did not mean she is completely helpless. Kitty has made several attempts to bite him.

The first few times that she tried to bite him were while he was undoing her ties. Teddy had simply laid his arm across her neck, cutting off her air supply ever so slightly. The next time she tried to bite him was as he was leading her back to the car after one of the bathroom breaks. He had her by the arm when she lunged at him, trying to bite his arm. He had let go of her on reflex and she had bolted. It did not take long for him to catch her and bring her to heel though.

Once they are in Chicago, Teddy finds a cheap hotel, just outside of the city proper. Paying in cash, he rents a small, run-down room for the two of them. He plans to getting a job with the ready-work crews and staying in the hotel until he can afford an apartment for the two of them. Kitty would not have to work, she could just stay in the hotel, relax and recover from the ordeals they had faced.

The following day, while Teddy is out, taking whatever work he could find through the ready work crews, Kitty is locked in the bathroom. He had untied her, believing that she is secure in the bathroom. The door is locked and the dresser is pressed against it. There is no way that she could possibly get out. Teddy had underestimated Kitty's determination.

As soon as Kitty is sure that Teddy had left the hotel room, she began working on the door. It does not take her long to get the door handle unlocked. It takes her a lot longer to push the door open, with the dresser in the way. She is lucky that the dress is empty. After hours of pushing, and with her legs and back burning from the effort, Kitty is finally able to get enough room between the door and the jam to squeeze through. She never looks back.

***

Teddy comes home to an empty hotel room. Kitty is gone. The dresser is still against the door but moved just enough to let her slip through. He has her shoes with him, as well as her clothes, so she had left barefoot and with absolutely nothing but the clothes on her back. He knows she would not be back though. She is gone. He is ruined.

Teddy figures that if she had managed to get to the police, they would have already met him in the hotel room. She must not have found a police station, or at least they must not have believed her. Either way, he has to act fast. Turning around, he goes back to his truck and leaves. He has paid for the first week's rent, but he just leaves it. There is no point in advertising that he is back on the move.

This time, instead of west, Teddy opts to head south. He is not sure where he is going to go, but anywhere is better than staying put, being a sitting duck. He is loath to leave Kitty, but she had left him first. He just hopes that she is going to be okay, but she is no longer his responsibility. She made the decision to go on her own. Whatever happens to her is beyond his control now.

This time he decides on a small town. Teddy also decides to start using a new name. He would claim that he lost his IDs, and take up residence with a new name. He would go by Charlie Green. He had served with a Charlie in Vietnam. He liked that guy. Green is a good last name, not common enough, or uncommon enough, to arouse suspicion. No one ever suspects a Green of anything.

It does not take long for Teddy to almost believe that he is Charlie Green. It took the town of Mansfield even less time to accept a Charlie Green into their community. He is soon hired to work the tractors on a farm and lives in a small cabin on the edges of the fields owned by the same farmer who had hired him.

Mansfield is not a dry community, but it is a sober one. There is a local bar, a couple of feed stores, and a supply store. There is a single gas station, a diner, a church, and miles of farmlands. The people there are a friendly, but a serious lot. They are wary of most visitors, but they welcomed Charlie.

Charlie Green makes sure never to let himself get drunk. He makes sure not to let people get too close to him. He knows that the greatest threat to his cover is himself. He can not afford to let anyone discover that he has ever been anyone other than Charlie Green. While it is a lonely life, it was a necessary life.

A Ghostly Goodbye — 2008

Maggie and Peter are sitting in the living room, relaxing with River. It has been a difficult few weeks. First, they found a dead body. Then they had to move in with Maggie's Mom while the police dealt with that body. Then they had gone ahead and paid for the burial of the child's body. Finally, they had to wait for the contractors to finish fixing the damage that had been caused by the police, hunting for any clues as to who that body belonged to.

To say that the small family needs some downtime is an understatement. Even River seems overly stressed by all of the activity that had occurred, even though she loved living with Maggie's Mom. Kathy loved to dote on River, often cooking for her like she was a human child. River has gained more than a couple of pounds in Kathy's care.

Maggie and Peter are on separate couches. After several weeks of sleeping together on a single couch, they are more than ready for a little bit of space to stretch their legs. River is sitting with Maggie, never ready to give up a single moment of cuddle time. River suddenly wakes from napping on Maggie's lap. She is staring hard at the landing by the stairs.

River's gaze is so intense that both Maggie and Peter looked up from what they are doing. Maggie had been reading a book, while Peter plays a game on his phone. River has not made a noise, but her interest is clear. There is something on the landing. Following her gaze, Maggie and Peter see it. They see the ghost of the child.

The apparition is translucent. They could see right through the little girl that now stands on the landing. Her blue dress tints the wall behind her, showing what color it was in life. Her blond hair had lost its definition, sitting like a cloud around her head. Only her face is well-defined, beautiful, and elf-like. Her blue eyes are still piercing, even in death. Maggie gasps in astonishment at what she was seeing.

As they stare at her, she develops a little more in detail. They can see her bare feet, one standing on the other. They can make out the small doll that she clutches, so like the one that they buried with her and exactly like the one that they burnt. They can even make out the small dimples that forms as she smiles at them. She gives them a small wave, as though to say goodbye. With that and an ever so slightly bigger smile, Annie's ghost moves on from the house she had haunted for so long.

"You saw that, right?" Maggie asks once the ghost had disappeared. River is still watching the landing as though the child's ghost might come back. Maggie watches the landing with her.

"Um, yeah. I think I saw what you saw. You saw a ghost, right?" Peter asks, confirming what Maggie had seen.

"Yep, a little girl ghost. I have got to assume that is the ghost of the child we found," Maggie says, finally looking away from the stairs and over to Peter.

"I should hope so. I would hate to think that there might be a second body here and that no one found it despite the police being here for days, looking."

"They would have found another body if there was one to find. They had cadaver dogs here, and everything. That had to be the ghost of the little girl," Maggie reasons. She has to convince herself, as well as Peter, that there is no chance of any other bodies in the house. It would be impossible to live there if there were any chance that a body might still be there.

"Did you see the little doll she had?" Peter asks.

"It looked just like the one we found on the steps, just newer, cleaner. It looked a lot like the one we buried with her."

"When I burned that doll, I thought I heard a scream. Like someone was screaming, 'no.' It might have been her. I might have ruined her doll," Peter remembers, feeling bad that he hurt this child, unintentionally.

"She did not seem like she was blaming us for anything. She looked happy, just before she disappeared. I think she felt the doll's sacrifice was worth it, provided it helped us find her. In a way, it did kind of help us. It told us something about her, and we did replace the doll," Maggie reminds him. She does not like to see him sad, even if it was over a doll and a ghost.

"Yeah. It makes me wonder if a lot of the weird things in the house were her trying to communicate with us. They had to have been. I wonder if she had tried this with other families, or if she was just waiting for someone like us."

"I don't know. It is a little late for us to ask her."

"Too bad neither of us thought to ask her what her name was. It would have made it a lot easier to find her family," Peter says with a little laugh.

"I'd love to watch you explain that one to the police. 'Hey, I know the girl's name and her parent's names. How? Oh, she told us.' I don't think the police would believe us," Maggie mimes the conversation with her hands, making talking motions and laughs.

"True, although it would have made it easier to try to find them in the papers at the library."

"Do you still want to hunt for her family?" Maggie asks. The ghost is gone, is it worth it to continue hunting, knowing that the police were already on the case?

"Yeah, I think we still owe it to her to do our best to find her family. If we do find anything, we can just turn that over to the police. They would know what to do with the leads that we dug up, and they would know how to handle the family," Peter decides.

"Okay, we'll keep looking," Maggie agrees.

Kitty — 1976

It takes her a while, but escaping the hotel bathroom is not half as difficult as escaping her home's bathroom. The lock on the hotel bathroom is designed to be opened from the inside of the bathroom, not the outside. Teddy did not think about that when he locked her in there, but Kitty realized it right away. She made a point to not twist the handle while she was hitting the door before he left. She did not want him to know she could escape.

What Kitty does not anticipate was the dresser in front of the door. The door swung out of the bathroom, into the bedroom. It is a safety hazard, for sure, but it is necessary with the design of the bathroom. Unfortunately for Kitty, it means that she has to work harder to secure her escape.

The dresser only gives the door a couple of inches of play before the door hit the dresser. It is not a lot, but it is enough. With the use of the shower curtain to act as a level and her own desperation to heighten her strength, Kitty pushes, pulls, and pries the dresser away from the door just enough to escape.

Once she is through the door, she begins to pillage the room for anything that would help her. She couldn't use the phone to call for help. It has no dial tone. She has no shoes, no wallet, and no money. She has only what was on her person. She does not even have a snack. Using the sink and her hands, she gets herself something to drink, then heads out the door. She would try the hotel's office first, and if that did not work, she would find a police officer. She would see Teddy arrested.

Kitty is careful to look around and make sure that Teddy is not in the parking lot before she left the hotel room. There is no point in getting caught by him at the very beginning of her escape. If he caught her, she is certain that he would tie her to the toilet or some other equally horrible restraint. Giving her freedom of movement while he was gone was a mistake that he would not make twice.

Once certain Teddy is not there, she walks quickly to the hotel office. She winces at the feel of the cement against her bare feet. She never went barefooted at home, and her feet are not used to the small stones and rough edges that they encounter. The greeting she gets from the hotel office is not what she expected.

"OUT!" shouts the man at the front desk. Kitty is not fully in the office when he starts yelling at her to leave.

"But, I need help," Kitty starts to say. Her eyes are wide in shock. She had expected a little bit of resistance, after all, she had no shoes on and she is certain that Teddy had not told them about her. She did not expect outright hostility.

"Nope. Out," The man shouts once again. He swings his hands in the direction of the door, shoeing her out. Kitty tries to protest, but he is not having it.

As she leaves, she hears him saying, "Streetwalker or lot lizard. It doesn't matter, they're all the same," to someone in the back. She is not going to get any help there.

Kitty decides that she would go with her second course of action, and try to find a police officer or at least a payphone. 9-1-1 is free to call, and this might not be an emergency any longer, but she certainly needs help.. She goes to the front of the hotel and looks down the street, in both directions. They both look equally bad. There are no stores, no parks, and no people to be found either way she looks. If it were a movie, it would be Alfred Hitchcock, it was so unsettling.

Turning to her right, Kitty starts to walk. She is careful with her feet. She avoids the glass when she can. She walks high on the balls of her feet, putting as little of her foot on the ground as possible. It is exhausting and slow going, but it is the best that she can do. She tries to wave down the few passing cars she saw, but no one stops. She can not blame them. She looks horrible.

She thinks that she had finally struck gold when a man asks her if she needed some help. He is a shifty-looking man, but she is a shifty-looking woman. She figures that if he was offering to help her, he could not be as bad as he looks to be. After all, she is evidence that looks can be deceiving.

"Yes, I could really use some help. My husband, he killed my daughter, and I need the police. I need..." Kitty trails off. He is taking her by the arm and steering her away from the street.

The man is a non-descript type of individual. Not much taller than Kitty. His hair is a dirty blond, and his eyes were grey-blue. There is nothing about this man that would stand out from any other man. This trait has helped him many times before. People can not remember the un-memorable.

"I'll help you. Why don't we just go to my apartment? You can call the police there, rest, and get cleaned up a bit. Your feet are bleeding," he offers. He smiles disarmingly at Kitty as he talks. She is too tired to fight him and the prospect of getting cleaned up and him helping her was too much for her to resist. She allows herself to be led away.

"It isn't far," the man says. "My name is Tim," he introduces himself. He leads her into an alley and he does not want her to get spooked and start fighting him. She might hurt herself.

"Tim. I'm Kitty," she answers. Her voice sounds distant to herself. It is as if she is going into shock. She keeps her eyes on Tim, not watching where they are going. She does not want to see where they are going.

Once they are deeper in the alleyway, Tim turns and looks her full in the face. "Sorry, chica," he says. He smiles sadly at her, then strikes. He stabs her in the chest, piercing her lungs. She is not even able to get a scream out before she is down. Unable to catch her breath, she tries to gasp, tries to call for help. Meanwhile, Tim is rummaging through her pockets, finding nothing, he slits her throat and walks away.

The Manhunt — 2008

While there are certainly cases colder than the one that Detective Damien Fields is working on, but this one was plenty old. This is the case with the little girl that someone found in their rafters. There is not a lot to go off on in this case. They have a body and a cause of death. They have an approximate year, but nothing remotely closer than that. Thirty-year-old crimes are rarely actually solved.

Detective Fields' first course of action is to determine who might have lived in the house at the time. He finds the former owner, Robin McGuire, and he found out that his father had owned the house before him. It had been a rental for most of the past thirty years. They do not keep records that far back. They do go above and beyond with their record keeping, keeping track of the financial and rental agreements for the past ten years, but that is only a third of the time that he needs.

Detective Fields begins knocking on doors. It is a long shot, but he was hoping that some of the homes in the neighborhood might have families that have lived there for a long time. He is very lucky when he came across a Bobby Bricher. He had grown up in his home and had taken it over for his parents when they got too sick to live in their home anymore.

Bobby had grown into a tall and well-built man. His dark brown eyes were warm and welcoming. His hair always looks like he had just gotten up, and his smile instills trust. At forty-four, he was just past his prime, but very far from old. He still remembers Annie. Answering Detective Fields' question about anyone who moved suddenly, he could clearly remember the family that used to live in the house.

"Oh yeah, I used to have a friend who lived in that house. Her name was Annie. I don't remember her last name, though. It was similar to an author I recently heard of, but I wouldn't be sure if I heard it again. Koontz maybe, but her last name could have been completely different. I was ten back then."

"Do you know what happened to the family?" Detective Fields asks. His nearly black eyes kept flipping back and forth from the notebook he was taking notes on, to Bobby, as they sit at Bobby's kitchen table, a cup of coffee each between them.

"I just know that they up and vanished one day. I didn't see them go. I just remember ringing their doorbell, wanting to play with Annie, but they weren't there. My parent's didn't see them leave, but they explained what it meant to skip out on rent and that Annie did not likely have a choice about it," Bobby answers, his eyes glazing over as he slipped into memory. He could picture the door and the house as he rang the bell. There was something else...

"I think there was a raccoon on the porch. A dead one. I remember thinking that was really weird and wondering why no one moved it off the porch. It stank to high hell, but at ten, I was not going near it," Bobby remembers.

"That's probably how they disguised the smell of the body in the rafters if the body of the little girl was their daughter. How old was Annie when you knew her?"

"Annie? She was a year younger than me. So she would have been nine. It would have been 1976," Bobby answers. He can still picture sweet, little Annie. He had really liked her.

"I hate to tell you this, but that would fit with what was found at your neighbor's house. As I am sure that you know by now, the body of a young girl was found in the rafters of their porch. It appears to have been there for the past thirty years or so. I think that body might be that of Annie's. Do you know anyone who might know the family's last name, or what her parent's names were?"

"Well, my mom is still around. She's over at the St. Jude Nursing Home, so we can swing by there and see if she remembers. Her body might be failing her, but her mind is still a steel trap. It's still early enough that she'd be awake and happy for the company. Wanna check it out?" Bobby offers. Detective

Fields agrees quickly. This could be the perfect lead that he is looking for.

***

Detective Fields follows Bobby up to the St. Jude Nursing Home. It is not far from where Bobby is living, just up a couple of streets. It is a nice, clean facility, attached to a Catholic Church. The nurses there are polite, and the residents looked clean and well-cared for. Everyone knows Bobby by sight and name, marking him as one of the few individuals who visits his family frequently.

Bobby's mother, Patricia, is indeed awake. How willing she is for visitors is a matter of debate though. She has just gotten into a new book. She has been waiting for this book for the past year, and it just came out that day. Setting the book aside, she smiles as she greets Bobby and Detective Fields. She makes sure that Bobby sees the book and knows that he has better feel lucky that she loves him so.

"Mrs. Bricher, I am Detective Fields. I was wondering if I could ask you some questions about your old neighbors. The ones that moved out suddenly in the mid-1970s?" Detective Fields introduces himself to Mrs. Bricher. He can tell immediately from just a glance, that this is a woman whose body might fail her, but her mind never would. She made him miss his own mother. Her situation had been the reverse of this woman's.

"The ones with the little girl that my Bobby liked so much? Oh yes, I remember them well," Mrs. Bricher answers, shocking both Bobby and Fields. That was in fact the family that they are looking for answers about.

"Yes, that family," Detective Fields stammers. He was not expecting to get answers this quickly.

"They were the Koonz family. K-O-O-N-Z. The father was a man by the name of Teddy, and the wife's name was Kitty. The little girl was Annie. He was a drunk and a bastard. Kitty was a sweet, but weak woman. They did not deserve Annie. It broke my heart when they pulled her out of school. It shattered it when they moved away so suddenly," Mrs. Bricher said. From the shell-shocked look on Bobby's face, he had never heard his mother talk so bluntly about anyone and never heard her call anyone a bastard.

"How do you remember them so well, Mama?" Bobby asks. He is completely taken aback by her recollection of them.

"Oh, honey, you were in love with that little Annie girl from the first moment you set eyes on her. It was so obvious. I had to learn about them even if just to protect you. If they'd have stuck around, you would have ended up with that little girl, and I would have ended up dealing with Teddy. A shotgun might have been the appropriate answer there. I remember how he used to beat Kitty. You could hear her screams all through the night. It was horrible. I begged her to let me help her, but there was nothing to be done. She wouldn't leave, and wouldn't take help," Mrs. Bricher shakes her head at the memories.

"Now, why don't you tell me why you want to know about such a family," Mrs. Bricher asks Detective Fields.

"Well, I think we found Annie," Detective Fields begins, explaining all that has been found and how it was found to the woman. It is almost like talking to his mother, before she got so sick and lost herself, and despite the horror of what he says, he feels better for talking to her. He will have to come back and visit just for the sake of visiting when all of this is over.

Remorse — 1977

Teddy Koonz, now known as Charlie Green, has been almost dry for a year. It has been a long year for him. He never thought that he could go so long without a drink, without alcohol to chase the nightmares of Vietnam away. He has tried before to go dry, for Kitty and for Annie. It never worked. The call of the bottle was always just too much.

Now, he is going dry for himself, and it might still be an uphill battle, but it is one that he is making. If only he could have figured out how to fight this battle before he made the worst mistake in his life. If only he could have figured it out before he killed Annie.

If he could have figured out a year ago how to avoid the drink, how to sink himself into blind work and then exhausted sleep, then his life would have been so much different than it was now. Gone were the days of coming home to dinner made by his beautiful wife, wherever she might be. Now his dinners are whatever he manages to scrounge together from what meager supplies he thinks to buy from the grocery store.

No longer does he sleep in a warm bed, side by side with his wife. Now he sleeps in a cot, just big enough for him. Yes, he managed to buy himself a blanket and pillow, but they are not like the ones that Kitty had found in that small boutique so many years ago. He remembera paying what felt like a small fortune for that bedding, and now he misses their comforts.

No longer does he come home to a house filled with sound and life. Now he spends his evenings in a silent shack, with no one and nothing for company besides himself. The trappings that make a house a home are nowhere to be seen. He is not so much as living as he is surviving. It is not the life he foresaw for himself. It is no less than what he needs, and far more than what he deserves.

All too soon, it becomes too much for him. The long and lonely days out working in the fields, followed by long and lonely nights in what he now called his home, are beginning to take a toll on him. He can almost hear the voices that he longs for calling to him. He would swear that he heard Annie's laugh in the corner, the sounds of her playing with her Dolly. He would crawl into bed and swear that he could smell the perfume that Kitty wore. It is more than enough to cause a man to want to lose himself.

***

Charlie does not want to get his first case of vodka from the local distillery, not that his town has a distillery. He has to travel a couple of towns over to get to one that has a liquor store. That alone would guarantee that he would not be buying too much alcohol. There is no way that he could make the trip more than a couple of times a month without being noticed. That is the problem with small towns, they all know each other and they all know each other's business.

Purchasing the case of vodka from the liquor store feels a lot like doing a crime to Charlie. He had to sit in the parking lot across from the store, watching it for fifteen minutes before crossing the street in his old truck. Once in there, he does not dally. He finds the first case of cheap vodka he could lay his eyes on and buys it. Putting it in the bed of his truck, he wraps it with a tarp. He has no intention of letting others see what he had bought. He feels the shame of his actions and the judgments of his neighbors. It is not enough to make him stop and reconsider his actions though.

When he gets home, he immediately unloads his truck. He does not want to leave the vodka out where anyone else might find it. He immediately puts it in a closet, under some spare blankets, all but one bottle. That one bottle he puts on the table, ready to drink, which he does not immediately do. Instead, Teddy, now known as Charlie, stares at that bottle for two hours. He just stares.

After two hours of staring at the bottle, he opens it, drinking directly from the bottle itself. The first pull immediately upsets his stomach. He has to bite back bile as his body rejects the harsh drink. Even when he was a heavy drinker, he had primarily stuck to beer. This was something altogether different and it has been a long time since he had drank at all.

It would have been reasonable for Charlie to stop there and rethink his behaviors. It would have been reasonable for him to dump the vodka and go to bed. It would have even been reasonable for him to abandon the bottle where it sat and find his solace in the sheets. He knows he will need to be up early, he knows that he is setting himself up for failure. He also knows he can still hear the snap of Annie's neck, and the screams of Kitty as he forces her to leave her dead daughter.

Gripping the bottle's neck tightly, as though to strangle it into submission, he bites the lip of the bottle as he sucks down another gulp. It is harsh. It is punishing. It is more violent than it needs to be, both him and the vodka. They fit each other well, and he knows it will destroy him. He almost wants it to destroy him. He is nothing more than a shell of a man, and if the vodka could not fill him, maybe it would shatter him.

Eyes swimming with drink and the bottle half empty, Charlie finally slumps in his seat, sleeping where he sits. It is the deep, dreamless sleep of the drunk, but not a restful sleep. The dawn comes fast and hard, streaming light through his windows and onto his face, bouncing off the bottle. This is the start of the end of his life, and Teddy, now Charlie, knows it.

Old Records — 2008

Detective Damien Fields makes sure to keep Peter and Maggie Reed up to date with everything that he has found about Annie Koonz and her parents, Teddy and Kitty. They have been so insistent on helping with the case that it keeps him motivated, even when he knows that he will be facing an uphill battle trying to find Kitty and Teddy. He is secretly hoping that they would be the ones to find the clue that would lead to Teddy or Kitty. They have been through so much with the case, that they deserve to be able to provide positive assistance.

It is very frustrating to find that it appeared that Kitty and Teddy Koonz all but fell off the planet in 1976. They do not show up in the city census, there are no tax files, and they are not in the news at any point. While Maggie and Peter focus on the local region, Detective Fields stretches his contacts out, searching the entire United States for the pair. He narrows down the years, thinking to pick up the trail and move forward, rather than back in locating Annie's parents and finding the truth as to what happened.

Keeping a narrow search field from 1976 to 1980, Detective Fields searchs for any arrest records for Teddy or Theodore Koonz. It takes a while, but he finally finds something in the small town of Shyne. It was an arrest record for one Teddy Koonz with an alias name of Charlie Green. It has the right social security number, matching Teddy Koonz's military record. He has found his man.

According to the record, Teddy had gotten drunk and picked a fight with an officer of the law while in Shyne. He had been living in a neighboring town, Mansfield. The same officer that he tried to fight with arrested him and held him for the night, releasing him back on his own recognizance with nothing more than a fine. It looked like he was on his way to Mansfield, Tennessee to see if he could pick up the trail.

***

Mansfield, Tennessee has not changed much in the time that Teddy had lived there through the time that Detective Fields arrives. The sheriff's office has expanded to a full state police barracks, there are a few more stores, and the farming machinery was more modern, but that was about the only change. To Detective Fields, it is like stepping back in time.

Detective Fields chooses to meet up with his contact, Detective Waters, at the local diner. There they discuss the details of the case or the severe lack of details, rather. While a name, age, and social security number can often seem like a lot to go off of, for someone who is accustomed to hiding, this could end up being a long and difficult hunt to find Teddy Koonz.

The easiest thing to do was to start with the farm that he had been working at, Detective Waters assurs Detective Fields. "The farm has been in the same family for generations. They would have someone who remembers anyone who lived on the property or worked for the family. We'll start there."

"Sounds good. I'll let you do the talking. They might know you better, and be more willing to answer your questions," Fields agrees.

"Sure thing. They're right up the road. Let's take my car. No sense in taking two of them to go to the same place," Waters suggests, dropping enough money to cover the bill and a nice tip onto the table that they were sitting at. With a wave at the waitress, they are out the door and on their way to the farm where Teddy had spent his time working at.

***

The main house of the farm is exactly what one would expect of a farmhouse. It is a white, two-story home with a wrap-around porch. There are quilts hanging off the railings of the porch, evidently put there for when the evenings get cooler. The whole place feels inviting. Fields immediately feels at home and he can see why entire generations stay on the property.

Mr. Hubbard happens to be at home when Waters and Fields knock on his door. "What did he do this time?" he asks, as he swings the door open for the two detectives.

Waters chucks, "Sorry, we're not here about Andrew, this time." Waters turns to Fields, "Andrew is Mr. Hubbard's youngest son. He always seems to be getting himself into some type of minor trouble. He's a nice enough boy, though. He never does anything major, just small things."

"Well, come on in, make yourself at home. Margie made pie and there is coffee in the pot," Hubbard says, leading them into the house. The whole home is inviting. There are toys scattered about from Hubbard's grandchildren. There are dogs lounging on the chairs, and cats sitting on the couches. The whole home is full of love and comfort. It is a comfortable place to be.

Leading them into the kitchen, Hubbard sits down with them at the kitchen table while Margie fusses about, getting coffee and pie, no matter what the answer to her offer is. One might have said no to pie, but they are getting some anyway.

"Mr. Hubbard," Waters starts, only to be interrupted by the man.

"I'll not answer a single thing if you call me that. I am Luke, and you know it. I know you prefer your last name to your first, Eugene, but I will not have you call me Hubbard. Luke, got it?" Luke points his finger at Waters.

"Loud and clear," Waters says with a smile. He calls Luke "Hubbard" just to tease him. This is something they do every time they get together. It initially put Fields on edge, but when he sees them joking, he relaxes, picking up on the teasing nature between them.

"Luke, back in the mid-seventies, there was a man who was working here, Charlie Green. Do you know anything about him?" Waters is leaning forward, towards Luke, watching him carefully.

"Well, that's not a name I have heard in a long time. Charlie Green. Yeah, I remember him. I was a kid mind you, a teenager really, when he came to work on our farm. He stayed down at the hunting shack by the creek. He shot himself there, too. He left some papers, a suicide note from what I understand. I think we still have it. I can show you where he is buried if you like."

"Yeah, we'd like that. And we'd like to see the suicide note, maybe the shack where he stayed if that hasn't been destroyed or renovated too much,"

Waters answers. This is not the answer they are looking for, but it is an answer. Hopefully, they would learn something from what this man left behind.

A Drunken Stupor — 1978

Teddy sits there at his kitchen table. It is the only table in the house. The house is only a shack. His life is in shambles, and all because of the drink and his temper. That does not mean that he is not wasted at his table, furious once again.

Teddy, who had been going by Charlie, has wasted his life. He has destroyed everything that was good around him and drove away anything good within himself. He feels that he can not even begin to develop anything of a relationship with anyone or anything, that he is a monster, and he might be right.

When the knock sounds at the door, it startles him into alertness, but not soberness. It is impossible to be sober with the amount of vodka he has drunk. Stumbling over to the door, he opens it quickly, hoping to startle any would-be attackers into faltering. It is the boy from the farm, Luke.

"What can I do for ya?" Teddy slurs. He is not used to seeing the owner's son in his home. They tend to keep away from him beyond giving him instructions as to what needs to be done on the farm. Teddy likes it that way.

"Pa wants to know if you want to come down for the July 4th celebrations. We're gonna have food and fireworks," Luke says, taking a step away from the door. The stench of vodka is strong on Teddy, not to mention the rank scent of old sweat. Teddy has not washed up for the day, but rather just started drinking as soon as he got in from the fields.

"Tell 'Pa' no thanks. I ain't no fan of fireworks," Teddy answers as he starts to close the door.

"Sir, are you drunk?" Luke asks. He does not mean to sound accusing, just curious. He has not seen anyone drunk before. The most his Pa ever had was a glass of wine with friends. They do not even have a beer or the hard stuff at the house.

"What's it to you?!" Teddy bellows back, lunging slightly forward toward Luke. His sudden movement causes him to lose his balance and stumble. It is enough to scare Luke though, he takes off running back to his house.

***

It feels like a couple of hours later, but it is less than thirty minutes before Pa comes by the shack. His knock is a stronger, harder version of Luke's. Teddy knows who it was before he bothers to get up and answer the door. Mr. Hubbard is leaning against the door jam, just to the right of the door when Teddy answers it. "Charlie, we gotta have a talk," he says, allowing his southern accent to draw out the words.

Teddy backs away from the door as Mr. Hubbard swings himself into the small house. Teddy shows him to the table and even pulls out a spare cup for him and pours him a shot of the vodka. It is not good, sipping vodka. This is the rough stuff that was only good for fast shots and heavy mixers.

Being of good manners, Mr. Hubbard takes a small sip of the vodka, pursing his lips so that none passes between them. Once Teddy sits down, he begins what he came down there to say. "Now, Charlie, I ain't got no problem letting you stay here and use this old hunting shack as a place to stay. We have done our level best to let you be, but there are going to need to be some changes."

Mr. Hubbard leans forward, looking Teddy in his vodka-soaked eyes, "I and the Mrs. have noticed a significant decline in your productivity and the quality of the work you have been doing. Just last week I had to re-till the entire lower field. All of the lines were wavy, making planting impossible. We weren't going to say anything, figuring you were just tired or going through something. But, I can now see what you are going through. We can't be having you working drunk or hung over. It isn't safe for you and it isn't productive for this farm."

Teddy doesn't say anything. He knows he has been messing up on the farm. He knows that it is because of the vodka. He knows that this job is on borrowed time. He knows he is on borrowed time.

Mr. Hubbard sits there for a bit longer, hoping that his words would sink into the man. It is hard getting good help, and for the most part, Charlie Green had been a good help. He does not want to have to lose the man. "If you need help, please let us help you. There's an AA meeting every Friday evening in the church's basement. I'd be happy to sponsor you. I've sponsored a lot of other gentlemen over the years," he tries one more time to get through to the man. He knows it is not going to take.

"Thanks, I'll think about it," Teddy answers. He knows that Mr. Hubbard is looking for something of a response. He does not want to promise to go to the meetings though. He has never wanted to go to those meetings, and now even less. What if those people learn his truths, that he is not Charlie Green, that he was married to Kitty, that he had killed his Annie?

Mr. Hubbard continues to look at Teddy for a couple of more minutes before he stands up. "I'll show myself out," he says as he walks out the door of the small shack. He can only hope that he has made a difference in the man's life and that he would at least clean up enough to be functional. He fears that he has not.

As the night wears on, friends, family, and farmhands dance, sing, and feast at the Hubbard's home. When the fireworks go off, everyone cheers, celebrating the birthday of their great nation. No one hears or notices the extra bang that echoes from the backfield. It had gotten lost in the sounds of celebration.

Hidden Bones — 2008

Luke leads Detectives Waters and Fields to the backfield. The old hunting shack is up against the back edge of the field. There are woods surrounding it on three sides, with the field against the back of the shed. It is a scenic area.

The shack is an old single-room designed house. It has grey wooden shingles and a wooden roof. There is ivy growing along the bottom part of one of the walls. The windows are open, and the door well hung. It was obvious that the house is still in use, even after all of these years.

"My kids like to hang out here sometimes. It gives them a break from being in the house and under their Mom's eye. I'd join them if I thought I could get away with it," Luke tells Waters and Fields as he walks towards the shack. As he speaks, they can see one of those children sticking their head out from the window.

"That's my daughter, Leah. She's a good kid. God help the man that she picks, though," Luke says, identifying the kid as she slips back in the window. He adds a little chuckle at the end of that to indicate that he is joking, at least almost joking..

Luke does not bother knocking on the door when they reach the shack. The kids inside already know that they are on their way over, Leah told them. The four that are in the shack all jump out, running and laughing when Luke opens the door. He smiles, watching them play. They take off into the woods, likely to cause mischief for the squirrels who live there.

"Well, this is where old Charlie lived. He had a cot where the futon is now. The table is the same table though. So is the stove, but the refrigerator is new.

Things wear out, we have to replace them," Luke says as he gestures to the meager items in the shack. It is not barren, but it is also not crammed with stuff. It has just enough to get by with.

"You said he shot himself here?" Waters asks.

"Yeah, I didn't see it mind, you. Not him killing himself, or when they found him. I just remember my parents talking about it. From what I understand, he put a tarp under the chair and shot himself in the head. It happened over the July 4th holiday, so it took a few days for someone to find him," Luke answers. "My Pa was the one who found him. He came looking for him after he noticed that the fields weren't getting plowed. He expected to find the place empty."

"You said he was buried around here?" Fields asks.

"Yeah. The police tried to find his family. No one ever came by to claim him though, so we got permission to bury him at the edge of the field. It seemed as good of a place as any. We don't have a pauper's cemetery or anything around here, you see. Pa took the backhoe out, dug a plot for him, and they put him there, casket and all. It's marked so no one is surprised if they find him. You wanna see it?"

"Sure," Waters answers for the two detectives. They are not learning anything from the shack, and they do not expect to learn anything from the grave site, but they would go to be friendly.

The grave site is not very far from the shack, not even a few minutes' worth of walking is needed. Looking back, they could still see the shed, and off a bit in the distance, the main house. The site itself is small, with nothing to indicate a body is buried there except for a small stone marker. There it has the name, 'Charlie Green' and under that, 'Theodore Koonz'.

"We found out that he had another name after he shot himself. The state boys found it when they were investigating his suicide. They said he even had a wife and kid, although we couldn't find them to tell them that he had died," Luke says, looking down at the small marker. It does not have any dates on it. It is just a simple, plain stone with the names. Simple, like the man who it marks.

"You had mentioned a suicide note?" Fields asks after staring at the marker for a moment.

"Yeah, it's back at the main house. We keep it in an envelope in a curio cabinet. We figured that there was always the possibility that someone might want to know what happened to him. I'm rather glad that we kept it now, with you two here," Luke answers, squinting against the sun at the two men. He turns and leads them back to the house.

Back at the house, Luke leaves them in the capable hands of Margie. She immediately plies the men with cookies and cider, not taking no for an answer. While they are enjoying their snacks, Luke manages to find the old, dusty envelope that Fields is hoping holds some answers for him.

"Now, I've not looked at this in many years. I don't rightly remember what is in it. But, here you go," Luke says, handing the envelope over to Fields.

Opening the unsealed envelope, Detective Damien Fields carefully removes the old notebook paper and begins to read.

I have not been a good man. I have failed in every way to be a good man. I have let everyone down. I'm done letting people down. I'm just done.

Kitty, I am sorry I left you in Chicago. I should have went out and looked for you. I got scared when I couldn't find you, so I just left.

Annie, Daddy is so sorry for hurting you. You were the best thing that ever happened to me, and I went and threw it all away. Please forgive me.

I just can't keep on living with these hidden bones I have.

The note does not offer very many clues as to what might have happened to the rest of the family, but at least Fields has a starting place in looking for Kitty. He is hoping that he might find her, but he is doubtful.

Final Moments — 1978

It has been four days after Mr. Hubbard had talked to Charlie. He has not seen him, or any movement by the back shack in those four days. That is not unusual for Charlie. He is a private man who keeps to himself. He is not known for hanging around outside or talking to people just to be social. He is known for getting his work done, though. The East field has not been plowed, and that is what Charlie was supposed to be working on.

Mr. Hubbard is going to have to check on him, and he knows it. He considers sending someone else to do it. There is a chance that Charlie has just forgotten or is not feeling well. It is not like Charlie has a phone out there to call the house if he is sick. There is no reason to suspect the worst. Something makes him think that he had better be the one to check on the man, though.

Mr. Hubbard goes right before lunch to check on Charlie. He takes the small cart that he drives around the farm with him, and drives right up to the shack's door. He can smell it before he opens the door, the stink of death. He is glad that he did not have anyone else come up here to check on him. He did not want his sons to have to experience finding that he knew he would find.

As he opens the door, the stench gets worse. It is the ripe stink of shit and the copper scent of blood, the type of smell that you never forget. There is the sickly sweet smell of rotting meat overlying all of that. The sound of the flies as they take to the air when he disturbs them was almost deafening in that small room. Mr. Hubbard immediately closes the door. Nothing would be gained by staying there.

He takes a moment before he gets back into his cart. He is not prone to getting sick at the sight of some blood, but that is a lot of blood. He feels the dizziness that proceeds throwing up sweep onto him. It takes him several deep breaths before he can get it under control.

Once he no longer feels dizzy, he gets into his cart and drives away. He would have to call the police from the main house. It is only a few minutes from the backfield to the main house, but it seems a lot longer to someone who had not seen that kind of devastation done to a human body in a long time.

Once inside, he begins looking for Mrs. Hubbard. He wants to make sure that she does not let any of the children, or farmhands for that matter, near the back shack. There is no reason for anyone else to see that mess. He does not tell her what he saw, just that Charlie Green was dead. His next move is to call the police.

Mansfield does not have a police force. There are simply too few people living in the town to make it practical for them to field a barracks. Instead, he calls the State Troopers. They send someone up to his farm quickly. Unfortunately, it is not done discretely, and everyone who is at the farm notices the police driving up the long driveway. Work halts for the day, with everyone distracted. Mr. Hubbard notices it, too, sending for his foreman to take everyone to the main house for coffee, and then to send them home. Work is done for the day.

The State Troopers follows Mr. Hubbard to the backfield's shack in the cruiser. It is just small enough to fit on the dirt track that surrounds the fields, provided that they go slowly. Not that Mr. Hubbard would have been too upset over a couple of tire tracks on his pristine fields.

The sight that presents itself to the troopers was the same as what Mr. Hubbard had seen. The State Troopers are luckier in that they knew what to expect. They put mint lip balm over their top lips and walk into the mess. They photograph everything and bag the suicide note that was found on the table. By the time the ambulance arrives to take the body to the morgue, they have collected the evidence they need and are ready to head out. The case is pretty straightforward, Charlie Green had shot himself.

Mr. Hubbard then has a mess to clean up. Yes, the police took the tarp that Charlie had laid down, and the tarp did help to contain the mess, but there is still a lot that needed to be cleaned if the place is ever to be used again. It would have been easier to simply tear down the building and rebuild it, but the shack has been on the property for generations. He is loath to let one man ruin it so that future generations could not use the same shack that he and his grandfather had hunted out of. Instead, he decides to clean it.

Mrs. Hubbard offers to help him clean the place, but he feels that it was his responsibility. While there is no evidence of it, he feels that maybe he had pushed Charlie into committing suicide with their little talk on the fourth. Sure, the suicide note mentioned a wife, Kitty, and a daughter Annie whom he had let down. But that is not to say that he was not the final straw that broke the camel's back. For that, Mr. Hubbard would take on the challenge of cleaning the place by himself.

As he cleans, he piles the personal things that Charlie had left behind, like blankets and clothes in a heap outside. Once all of that is out of the way, Mr. Hubbard douses it with the rest of the case of Vodka that he had found tucked in the closet, and lit the whole thing on fire. If anyone came looking for it later, he would tell them what he did. But there was nothing worth saving and nowhere to keep anything. Mr. Hubbard even burns the cot that Charlie had been sleeping on, and the chair he had shot himself in. Soon it is as if he was never there.

The Final Moments — 2008

etective Damien Fields does his absolute best to track down Kitty Koonz. She is certainly no longer alive in Chicago, and while there is a chance that she might be somewhere else in the world, Detective Fields feels that it is unlikely. It is far more likely that she was one of the hundreds of Jane Doe's that were found murdered over the years in Chicago. That does not mean that he would stop searching for her, though.

With what little information he is able to gather about Kitty, and the answers he found about Teddy, Fields is finally able to make his final report and close the case. It is an unsatisfactory ending to the case though. Fields would have liked to have known that the guilty parties paid for their crimes against an innocent child. Instead, he will have to go with the suicide note and the knowledge that Teddy, at least, felt the shame of his actions.

When he turns in his report to his police chief, he is allowed to go home and relax after a challenging case. For Detective Fields, home is a small two-bedroom apartment with a cactus. Instead, he goes to the Reeds' home. He has to share the news as to what he found with them, as well.

When Maggie Reed answers the door, she is pleasantly surprised to find Detective Fields standing there. She burst into a smile that lit up her eyes, as she let him into the house. They have decided to stay in the house that they bought, rather than selling the house.

"You decided to stay?" Fields asks as he sits down at the kitchen table, gladly accepting a cup of coffee. Maggie makes a great cup of coffee.

"Yeah, I think the ghost moved on after we discovered her body," Maggie says, not mentioning that they knew that was the case because they had seen her move on. Peter still is hesitant to admit that was what he saw, even after admitting what he saw at the time.

"And having found a body in the rafters, and knowing there had been a murder here, doesn't bother you?"

"No. The body is gone, and you guys checked to make sure there were no more bodies, so that's done. As for a murder occurring here, yeah, we know it happened, but that was a long time ago. A lot of old houses have had people die in them, and quite a few of them have had murders. That stain does not stick to the house, just to the people who do it," Maggie answer, finally sitting down at the table herself. Peter walks in as she is taking her first sip of coffee and stands, leaning against the doorframe.

"Well, I have some news to share with you guys, regarding the body and the little girl's family," Fields begins once everyone is settled. "The little girl's name was Annie Koonz. She would have been nine years old when she was killed, most likely by her father, Teddy Koonz. We're not sure of the motive, but it easily could have been a horrible accident.

"Teddy, and his wife Kitty, skipped town right after Annie was murdered. They appear to have gone to Chicago, first. That is where the couple separated, with him leaving Kitty in Chicago while he went south, to a small town called Mansfield in Tennessee. He lived there for a year before taking his own life.

"Unfortunately, I don't know what happened with Kitty. She disappeared while she was in Chicago. The only information we have about her comes from Teddy's suicide note where he apologizes to her for leaving her there. It might be safe to say that she perished shortly after arriving in Chicago, although I don't know that. I will continue to look for her, but I have very little hope of finding her."

Detective Fields is very straightforward about what he found. He does not weigh down the couple with the various details of the case. He does not talk about the personalities of the people involved or about those who might have known the family. It is not their concern to get to know anyone else who is related to the case. He simply wants to provide closure to the family so that they can move on.

Fields is happy that the Reeds were staying in the home they bought, despite the grizzly things that they found in it. They seem to belong in the house. He hopes the love that they seem to share would be enough to cleanse the house of the darkness that had occurred there.

Once he is done telling the family about the end of the case, filling in minor details of how he found out the fates of the family members, without releasing his informants, it is time for him to go home. He excuses himself and walkes to the door with Kitty following him out to lock it behind him.

Fields stands on the porch for a minute, looking around. The Reeds have done a lot to repair the porch so that it looks like nothing had ever happened there. That is when he sees her. She is standing right next to him, simply appearing out of thin air. She is smiling up at him. He can not make out the color of her eyes or the tint of her hair, but her dress is blue. She is also translucent, lit with a glow from within.

Fields could have jumped, he could have felt fear, instead, he feels relief. He is not known for being superstitious, and he never advertises that he believes in ghosts. Instead, he keeps that to himself. Looking at the ghost of Annie, he is glad that he believes. He is glad that she appears happy, and he hopes that she would move on. After all, there was nothing else for her in this world. She has been found and the truth is hopefully known about what happened. She could rest.

Smiling back at the ghost, Fields turns and leaves the porch, turning his back on another case well solved.

II

Part Two

Annie

I died thirty years ago. I don't remember dying. I remember the moments surrounding my death though. I remember helping my Mom wash the dishes after dinner. I remember that Dad was in a very grumpy mood. He was drunk, something that he had not been for the past month. We had just finished dinner, and Mom was doing the dishes. I was helping her. I was being on my best behavior so he did not get too mad at me.

The last thing I remember from when I was alive was accidentally dropping a stack of plates. Then there was a flash of white. That was it. I don't remember Dad hitting me. I don't remember him breaking my neck. I don't remember any pain or even surprise. I just remember that flash of light.

The next thing I remember is watching Mom screaming my name, while she held my body. It felt very weird looking at myself, disconnected from myself, if that makes any sense. I tried to go to her, but I felt rooted to where I stood, even though I did not feel like I was standing at all. When Dad grabbed her and dragged up upstairs, I was suddenly able to move, like his movement reminded me how to do it.

When Dad locked Mom in the bathroom, I went with her. I tried my best to comfort her and tell her that everything was going to be okay. She could not hear me though. I tried to hug her, but she could not feel me. I felt her though, so I stayed close to her for a while. Eventually, I got curious though and tried to see what I could do.

It took me a while to figure out how to go through the door and out into the hall. All my life, doors were solid, so convincing myself to just walk through it was a challenge. What made it worse was that if the door was not solid, what made the floor solid. I spent a lot of time wondering why I did not just sink through the floors and into the ground. I still don't have a good answer for that and I have had a long time to think about it.

I watched as Dad put my body in the porch rafters. I kept looking around, but I could not see a single light at any of the neighboring houses, not that I had a plan for going to those houses and getting their attention. Mom did not see me, why would anyone else? I watched him bury my clothes. I watched him throw away my pictures. It was almost as if I did not exist anymore. My room and furniture were still there, but the details, the personality were gone. I was gone.

I watched with horror as Dad packed his and Mom's stuff in bags, and those bags into the truck. He was going to leave me, and take Mom with him. When he put Mom in the truck and drove away, I tried to follow them. I got as far as the neighbor's house before I felt my grip on this reality get loose and I was forced to turn around. I was afraid to see what would happen if I lost my grip on this half-life.

I don't remember being offered a choice as to what to do after I died. I just remember being next to my body, looking down at my Mom. But even if I was offered a choice, what other choice could I have made? I was just a kid. Between the options of staying with my Mom or going off to the unknown, of course, I would pick my Mom. What child wouldn't? But that also meant that I did not know what would happen if I lost touch with myself or this world. Would I go to heaven? Would I cease to exist? Would I go to hell? I was not a very religious child, and sometimes I could be bad.

Returning home, I cried. I lay down in my parents' bed and cried. I did not cry because I was dead. I did not cry for the hurt that my Dad caused me or for fear of my mom. I cried because I was scared. I was alone, truly alone, and no one could help me.

When Bobby showed up a couple of days after Dad left with Mom, I did my best to talk to him, to tell him what happened. I stood there, next to him, and screamed for all that I was worth. I even went as far as to grab his arm. I thought I had gotten through to him when he turned towards me, but he was just looking at the raccoon Dad put on the porch to distract people from me. There was another one under the porch, but Bobby did not notice that one. He tried a few more times to see if anyone was home, but I did not try to talk to him after the first time.

I might not have gotten through to Bobby, but I did learn something very important. I learned that I only had so much energy. While standing there and trying to get someone's attention was not very difficult when I was alive, now that I am dead, it was very taxing. I felt exhausted. I was able to sleep, but there was no food, so I could not eat, not that I felt the need to eat. Sometimes I miss eating.

More than eating, I miss dreaming. Like I said, I can sleep. I simply lay down where ever I want to, and fall asleep. I no longer feel cold, or hot for that matter, so I don't worry about blankets. I can just will my clothes to change, so that I am comfortable, so one less thing for me to worry about. When I sleep, it is dreamless sleep. I awake feeling rested, but I can feel the loss nonetheless.

When the landlord came by, I did not even bother trying to get his attention. I had never seen him before, in life, and he looked very distracted, going through the things that Dad left behind. He also looked angry, and I had never had a single good experience with an angry man. I was pretty sure that he was not going to be the person who could help me. I resigned to wait. I knew he would bring in new renters, eventually.

As family after family came into the home, I learned a few additional things. The big one was that if the family was loud or busy, there was no way that they were going to notice me. I could have formed fully corporal and walked through the house naked, and it would not have surprised some of the families that lived there, they were so busy. Instead, it was best to save my energy for times where the house was quiet, and for those families that were more calm.

I was pleased to discover that animals were able to see me. Dogs and cats, as well as the few ferrets I met, were all able to see me. Not only that, but they were able to interact with me. It was a great comfort to be able to cuddle with a pet when the rest of the family had gone to sleep.

Most of the families that I met in the years between my death and the Reeds coming to live in my house, I did not bother to interact with. They were all busy, and had excuses for anything that I might do to call attention to myself. There was one notable exception though.

There was a family, I forget their name, who had a son and a daughter. The daughter was nice, forgettable. The son was something else though. He had a mean streak that would put my father's to shame. He made it a point to torture animals, cats in particular. I made it my mission to destroy him and get his activities found out.

His name was Matt, but he liked to be called Syn. I don't know why, but that is not important. He would catch cats in wire traps, then torture them to death. He did some of the most horrible things you could think of to these poor animals. I did things back to him. I flooded his room with blood every night. It was really ectoplasm, or something, and was gone by the time the sun rose and there were no stains. I dragged his victims out into the open for others to find. I cut his traps and sabotage his tools. Eventually, he got caught and had to go away to a hospital. I slept for a year. It was worth it.

I knew that the Reeds were different than other families that had come through the house. For starters, they were not renting the home. They had bought it. For thirty years, everyone who stayed at my home were renting it. Not the Reeds though, they opted to buy the house. The other thing was that they did not have children.

At first, I was very confused as to what a young pair of adults were going to do with a five-bedroom house. They managed to fill it though, and not with children like I expected. Instead, they had crafting rooms, a library, a workout room, and a lot of living spaces. The house felt warm and comfortable, and not like just a launching point.

Another important difference between the Reeds and the other families I met was their demeanor. They were calm people. They moved deliberately and were not prone to excessive emotional bouts. That made it a lot easier to try to communicate with them. It is easier to talk when it is quiet than it is to be heard when it is loud. I started to make a plan.

The first part of my plan was to let them know that I was there. I started that by opening all the cabinets in the kitchen. I had seen that trick on the television shows that some of the previous families liked to watch. I then played with the lights, another trick I picked up from the TV.

Then I had to convince them to care about me. I showed them who I was, how young I was, and gave them hints about my personality. I found my doll and showed it to them. I showed them the pictures that Bobby and I made together. I wrote them a note asking for help and warned them when mice were around. I listened as they talked together, and I knew it was working. They were believing, and they cared.

The final phase of my plan was to show them where I was hidden. That was a lot harder than I expected it to be. Lifting the ground up so that my clothes could be found was a challenge. The cement did not want to move. I spent months lifting it. I slept for months after I got it moved. Showing them where my body was, was an accident. The slats fell on their own when the tree branch fell. I was very grateful for that.

When Maggie and Peter Reed buried me, giving me a good place to rest, I felt like I finally had a real chance to move on. I no longer felt afraid of moving on. Because of some weird trick of being dead, I could now be at the cemetery or at home. I was able to see myself buried. It was rather nice. I still did not feel like I was ready though, so I decided to wait. I pushed myself hard though, and let Maggie and Peter see me that evening, and I got to say goodbye to them. I think they needed it.

Detective Damien Fields was the last person to see me before I crossed over. He had worked so hard to find out who I was, and who my parents were. He wanted for there to be justice for my death. In a way there was though, Dad had just delivered it to himself. I wish I knew what happened to Mom though. I think Dad might have killed her, too. I know that she would never have stopped fighting him.

Detective Fields took the case personally. He spent a lot of time working on it. He would often drive by the house, or stop and look at it, even when he was supposed to be doing something else. When he came by to give his final report, I knew I had to show myself and let him know that I was grateful for his help. I willed my favorite dress and did my best to form my features, smiled, and waved. I think it was a good send off for both of us. As soon as he turned around, I let myself go. I was ready to move on.